Bedded Under The Christmastide Moon

Christina McKnight

PRAISE FOR CHRISTINA MCKNIGHT'S NOVELS

THE THIEF STEALS HER EARL
"When I started reading this book I could not put it down...it caused another book-hangover for me. I wanted to see how things would go when the truth of Judith came out and how Simon was going to handle it...loved it."-*Sissy's Book Review*

"Jude and Cart's story is such a delight! So refreshing to see the hero shy, socially awkward and not super wealthy. I love it...This was definitely one of the best books I've read this summer." -*Reviews from a Thrifty Mom*

FORGOTTEN NO MORE
"This author has made me love historical romance again." -*TwinsieTalk Book Reviews*

HIDDEN NO MORE
"The storyline was really good, the writing was great. So smooth and engaging, I was able to zip right through the story, it flowed so well. I love finding new to me authors and with this wonderfully written story by Ms. McKnight I've found a new historical romance author."-*Bound by Books*

CHRISTMAS EVER MORE
"*Christmas Ever More* was a wonderfully written festive novella full of hope, renewal, love, and new beginnings. If you're a fan of Christina's Lady Forsaken series, this is a must. Even if you aren't caught up, this stands well enough on its own to be a lovely addition to your holiday reading list."-*Literal Addiction*

BOOKS BY CHRISTINA MCKNIGHT

DEDICATION

For those who believe love never dies

PROLOGUE

October 1828
Hertfordshire, England

MISS MELLORIA STEELE, only daughter of the Baron and Baroness Montfort, stood before the small gathering in the gardens of her soon-to-be new home at Hockcliffe Manor. Her hands were damp with nerves as she clutched her bouquet of blue flowers to her chest. The light blue ribbon tied about their long stems matched the morning sky overhead. Mellie thought it fitting the hues were aligned in such a manner, as if the person collecting the blossoms and ribbon—likely Mrs. Gregston, the Hockcliffe housekeeper—had known the day would dawn without a cloud overhead. The tiny pin used to keep the bouquet tightly bound pricked the palm of her hand, and it was a welcome pain that helped to remind her this was not a dream.

She was fully awake. After this morning, nothing in her life would be as it was.

No longer would she simply be the lowly daughter of an impoverished baron, but something far more—yet also much less.

She glanced over her shoulder, the long waves of her cherished hair falling to cascade down her back as she spied her mother sitting tall and proud though forced, a weak smile upon her lined face as she attempted to keep her agony at bay until after the ceremony was complete. The woman's looks were nearly identical to her only daughter's with her blond hair tinted with hints of red and her almond-shaped green eyes; however, the Dowager Lady Montfort appeared twenty years older than her mere forty years of age.

The sickness did that to a person—and with rapid speed.

As evidenced by Melloria's father's quick decline into poor health and eventual death.

Had it only been a fortnight since she, her mother, and Lord Whitmore stood watch as her father was laid to rest at the Montfort family burial plot?

To Mellie, it seemed a decade ago, yet also just that same day.

Giving her mother a reassuring smile, Mellie turned back to the man before her.

Viscount Whitmore, Brigham Clarke…her childhood friend, neighboring lord, and the man she'd loved since before she was old enough to know what love entailed.

Her vision blurred as tears stung, threatening to escape long before the ceremony concluded.

She would not cry.

She would not allow anyone to see that her tears were not borne of happiness but of deep sorrow and regret.

A male throat cleared somewhere in the small gathering of witnesses, and Mellie scanned the crowd, her eyes alighting on the vile man who'd arrived on the eve of her father's death to claim the Montfort estate and destroy her entire world—not that it hadn't already been crumbling beneath her since the sickness took her father's ability to breathe without a cough or stand on his own. She would not address her distant relative by name, nor give him the satisfaction of knowing he'd given her no other option but to ruin Lord Whitmore's life as her cousin had ruined hers.

Mellie stood before Brigham, and a dozen witnesses, as the Hockcliffe vicar's stern voice echoed over the garden, speaking of obedience, honor, and deference.

Both Mellie and Brigham, as well as Mellie's mother, knew the truth behind this rash morning wedding. It was not because Brigham loved her. It was not because Mellie was making a vow to obey and honor Brigham. It was neither humbling himself or herself before the other in the presence of some deity Mellie was not certain existed. It was solely because without the union Mellie and her mother would be homeless, penniless, and without resources. The physician her family had employed since her father took ill had been released as soon as her cousin arrived, thus ending the baroness's care.

Without Brigham and this marriage, Mellie's mother would certainly perish within a month's time.

And so, Mellie stood before the man she'd loved since childhood, in her finest dress with matching slippers, her hair hanging free down her back with lengths of cream and blue ribbon weaved throughout her long curls, accepting his offer of marriage. And destroying the hope of any future either of them could have had if fate hadn't stepped in and crushed it.

She'd been skeptical and confused—and then grateful and sad—when Brigham had asked for her hand on the day her father was buried.

There had been no declarations of love, commitment, or devotion to one another...only a promise of a home and medical care for her mother.

When he made his gracious offer something inside Mellie had died. Her hope for love withered. The boy who'd tenderly wrapped her injured knee when she'd fallen from a tree, the man who stole a kiss from her one evening after their families had shared a meal, and the lord she'd dreamed of one day wedding, would be her husband in truth in a few moment's time.

...but in name only.

Their marriage one of convenience and borne of necessity.

Mellie glanced at the moss-covered stones under their feet, and a single tear slipped down her cheek, landing on her bouquet. She brushed the moisture trail, her hand shaking, glad the tear hadn't marred her gown.

Brigham shifted from foot to foot, his nervous energy evident. Did he realize the grave mistake he was making? She should have gone to him at first light and begged him to rethink his offer. Her life was over, but his need not be.

With time, Mellie would have solved the dilemma surrounding her cousin's shocking arrival and her and her mother's subsequent harsh ejection from her family home—Tapton House.

Yes, she loved Brigham with her entire heart—or at least what was left—but she'd never found the right moment to tell him. After her father's death and her cousin's arrival, she knew with certainty any declaration of love would be inappropriate and dismissed as words uttered due to her aggrieved state of mind.

"Mellie?" Brigham whispered in that soothing tone that was his alone. Light but nonetheless masculine.

She brought her gaze to meet his as he dragged his fingers through his curling hair and pushed it behind one ear. His hesitant smile and wide eyes made all the larger by his round spectacles gave her pause. In another lifetime, Mellie would have been happy and content to lose herself in Brigham's dark brown eyes every day.

Had the vicar asked something that was lost due to Mellie's wandering thoughts?

When Brigham continued to stare at her, Mellie glanced at the vicar, who also had his glare trained on her.

Without thought, she nodded.

The wide smile that appeared told her Brigham was satisfied with her answer.

Suddenly, their meager gathering of guests stood and clapped, smiles beaming from every direction, except that of her newly acquired cousin, the new Baron Montfort.

Brigham leaned toward her, and his lips grazed hers quickly before he took her bouquet and handed it to a waiting servant.

His smooth hand took hers, though she could not actually feel his skin through her cream-colored gloves. As a pair, they turned toward the waiting crowd.

Behind them, the vicar announced loudly for

all to hear, "May I introduce Viscount and Viscountess Whitmore."

Mellie attempted to smile for their guests, but it traveled no farther than her lips. Her green eyes held no twinkle. Her chin was not held high. And her cheeks were not the rosy hue of an excited woman ready to start her new life as a wedded lady.

Persephone Duggan—Brigham's elder sister—and her husband clapped with unbridled joy, their two young children joining in. As another friend of Mellie's, Brigham's sister had been overjoyed at the news of their betrothal and upcoming nuptials—so much so that she and her husband had packed up their small family and hurried to Hertfordshire to witness the blessed event.

Even her mother stood with the help of Mellie's maid, Lilly, and applauded.

No one present was deluded as to the reason behind her and Brigham's hasty marriage, yet that did nothing to diminish their joy over the union.

Mellie only wished she felt a fraction of their good cheer.

Brigham's hand tightened around hers. "You are trembling, Mellie."

She kept her eyes focused on their guests to keep from looking him in the eyes, for he was the one man who knew her well enough to reach through any excuse she uttered and see she was withering within.

"I cannot believe this is done, we are wed." *And that you gave up any chance of finding love on your own terms for me.* There was little hope she'd ever be in a position to repay his kindness or be worthy of all he was giving her. "I will see to my mother before we retire to the house for our meal."

When she started to pull away, Brigham kept a firm hold on her hand. "Are you certain you and the dowager will not accompany me to London? There are well-educated physicians in town, and I will have your mother set up in my townhouse. You will want for nothing. My sister and Saxton live close, and you will have a friend."

Mellie shook her head, glancing back at him. "My mother will not make the journey to town."

"Perhaps in a month or two?"

"The sickness only grows worse. You know that, Brigham." Which he did know…they both knew. They'd lived the awful fate of her father along with her sire. Each day, the baron's cough had grown worse until he could not so much as wheeze without blood staining the cloth he held to his mouth. Brigham hadn't borne witness to it every day, but he'd journeyed home from London at least once a month. "She is comfortable here, and the servants are as close as family. I would not wish for her to spend her final days in a foreign city, surrounded by strangers."

Mellie couldn't bring her eyes to his. She didn't wish to see the disappointment that likely lingered there. She'd noticed it since she agreed to wed him but remained steadfast in her decision to stay at Hockcliffe Manor. It wasn't her family home, but it was a place she and her mother were very familiar with. Even the servants had known her family for decades.

"When will you depart?" She pulled her hand from his grasp and let it fall to her side.

"After our wedding feast." He pushed his round glasses up on the bridge of his nose. It was a habit Brigham had done since youth—one she would have teased him about only a few years prior. "I have the bill to—"

Mellie held up her hand. "You need explain nothing to me."

"Persephone, Saxton, and the children will depart with me." Brigham glanced over her shoulder at the crowd that was likely dispersing, making their way toward the great hall where a small celebration was to take place for the new couple.

Brigham sighed as he clenched and unclenched his hands in front of him.

"Is there something else?" Mellie asked.

"If you do not wish me to depart, I can delay..."

"No." Mellie crossed her arms to keep from reaching out to him, begging him to stay, holding him, and not letting go. She was not a selfish woman and saw no reason to keep Brigham here only to play nursemaid to Mellie's mother. "You have important matters to attend to in London. I will not keep you from that. You were kind to return when my father's situation grew grave, and compassionate to a fault in giving my mother and me a home. I can ask nothing more of you."

Brigham shifted from foot to foot, much as he had in their younger days when he knew he'd done something to anger his father.

"If I cannot convince you to accompany me to London, and you have no need of me here at Hockcliffe, then there is nothing further to discuss."

Mellie feared that would be the way of things.

"I will see to my mother now." She turned to

find that most of their guests had indeed made their way inside, leaving only Mellie's maid and Mellie's mother seated in the front row of chairs. She closed her eyes for a brief second, pleading with herself to find some speck of happiness within her—at least for her mother's sake.

The Dowager Baroness had lost her husband, her home, and now would be forced to live with the reality of her only daughter wedding a man solely to provide adequate healthcare for her.

In life as a whole, her mother suffered far worse than Mellie ever would—and she'd do well to remember that.

CHAPTER 1

December 1833
Hertfordshire, England

LADY MELLORIA WHITMORE stood on the ridge that served as the dividing line between Hockcliffe land and her family home, Tapton House. The frigid December cold had long ago numbed her face. The sweeping winds pulled her skirts back toward Hockcliffe but blew her hair in the direction of Tapton House.

Which was very fitting, for Mellie was a woman torn between two lands, two lives, and two choices.

She breathed deeply, allowing the numbness to overtake her and banish the shivers that traveled down her spine. The punishing weather was soothing, in a way. It gave her something to focus on instead of the decision she need make.

Pulling her cloak tighter, Mellie thought

about reaching up to return her hood to its place. It would not do to become ill on the eve of Brigham's arrival for their Christmastide celebration.

Not that there had ever been much of a celebratory mood since they wed.

However, this year was different.

Tilting her chin skyward and closing her eyes, she allowed what little sun seeped through the patchy clouds to kiss her face.

Yes, everything was different.

She knew she should return to the manor and complete the preparations for Brigham's arrival, but Mellie lingered ever longer.

Bringing her stare back to her childhood home, her heart ached to see the destruction of the Montfort land and, in the far distance, Tapton House, abandoned for nearly three years now. Her cousin had come, threw her and her mother from their home, plundered the land for all its coal, and then fled when the property was no longer of value to him. The land was barren, and the house in disrepair.

No longer was it her home, either.

Not that her mother ever had the strength to make the short journey to Tapton House after her cousin abandoned the estate; however, Mellie was certain it had been the thing to push her the final step toward death. Her mother's home, where she'd raised Mellie and spent every moment dedicated to her husband, was gone forever.

Her mother had been gone for five months now—though it felt like years.

Mellie, with several Hockcliffe and Tapton servants at her side, had laid her mother to rest beside her father.

And now, Mellie would be facing Brigham

for the first time in nearly a year without the all-consuming burden of caring for her mother. Persephone and Saxton would not be joining them this holiday due to the impending birth of their fourth child.

It would be only Brigham and her.

Why did that terrify her so much?

But Mellie knew the answer; hadn't any doubt why this Christmastide season was so very different than the five previous holidays.

Melloria, Viscountess Whitmore, planned to seduce her husband.

As if the cold winter day agreed with her decision, the winds grew in strength, reassuring Mellie and reaffirming she'd chosen the correct path.

She'd loved Brigham at one point—many, many years ago before fate intervened, and she'd had to suppress her own longings to care for her ailing parents. Over the years, her girlish affection for him had been overpowered by her grief and loss.

But that obstacle no longer existed.

A certain measure of freedom had come the day her mother passed.

Mellie once again suppressed her feelings of guilt over embracing that freedom.

Caring for her mother hadn't been a burden, it had been her duty as a daughter. She would have stayed by her mother's side another ten years if it had been needed.

She could not blame her mother—or her father—for the course her life had taken.

Although, she did blame herself for stealing Brigham's chance at love.

The time had come to at least attempt some form of repayment. And that left Mellie with two choices: consummate her marriage and give Brigham an heir, or step aside and allow him to find a wife who could.

A wife who could both love him and give birth to another generation to continue the Whitmore line.

Mellie recognized the selfish choice of her decision.

Providing an heir also meant the end of her loneliness.

A baby would need care, and Mellie would dedicate herself to that task.

She could no longer allow Brigham to live as he had for all these years. It was past time Mellie gave back some of the kindness, compassion, and sympathy he'd shown her.

Lifting her chin, her conviction strong, Mellie turned away from her past...and looked to her future.

Hockcliffe Manor lay in the distance, nestled in a large grove of willow trees.

It had been her home for over five years, yet everything about the manor had changed in the last several months. The mourning period was still upon everyone, but the smell of sickness had been banished from the house, the windows thrown wide in every room without regard for the chill outside, and though she could not see it from this distance, Mellie had hung a wreath of holly on the front door. The servants no longer tiptoed about the house, and Cook no longer prepared broth for every meal.

It was Mellie who led the household into a new type of mourning, one free of grief and sorrow, it was the cloud they'd all lived under since she and Brigham wed.

Mellie started down the hill toward the manor, her gait not one of heaviness and burden, but light and confident.

Brigham had sent word the prior week that he'd arrive at Hockcliffe Manor on Christmastide Eve, as his reform bill was to be voted on before Parliament recessed for the holidays and the new year.

She looked to the road Brigham would use when coming from London.

How long would he stay this year?

As if her musings had conjured him from thin air, a lone figure on horseback appeared, a trail of dust in his wake as the rider leaned close to the animal's neck and raced toward Hockcliffe.

Brigham was home a day early.

Mellie took her hands from the deep pockets of her cloak and pulled her hood over her wild curls before lifting her skirts and sprinting toward the manor.

BRIGHAM SLUMPED FROM his horse outside Hockcliffe Manor, his eyes blurry from the dust of his travels as he attempted to focus on what hung from the front door. It was green and red—and very large—but squint as he might, he could not bring the thing into clear focus. He reached into the pockets of his coat, but they were empty. Next, he tried his trouser pocket and found what he searched for. Placing his rounded spectacles on the bridge of his nose, Brigham noted the thing appeared to be a wreath of some sort, evergreens mixed with holly and plump, red berries.

He hadn't seen a wreath adorn the door of Hockcliffe in many years.

Giving his head a quick shake, Brigham turned to collect his bag that was tied to his gelding.

The journey from London had left him tired, filthy, and chilled to the bone. The only saving grace had been the lack of precipitation; muddied roads would have made the trip far more perilous, and risked his horse's safety as well as his own.

There had been no need to rush out of London and push his steed at breakneck speeds, only to arrive at Hockcliffe and confess to Mellie that he'd failed. It wasn't so much that he'd failed, but that his bill calling for stiffer regulations for coal mine operations did not make it to a vote. Two years—incalculable hours spent meeting with lords all across England— championing a much-needed reform bill, only to have it cast out before Brigham could even speak to Parliament at large.

Bloody hell, but he'd had to miss Mellie's mother's funeral because he'd been in Dover courting Lord Caruthis as if he were a bloody innocent debutante...and Brigham in need of a rich wife.

And in the end, he'd disappointed Mellie once more.

Looking her in the face would be impossible knowing he'd failed her.

Brigham leaned his forehead against his horse, the animal's heated skin a welcome sensation against his chilled face.

Perhaps it would have been best to call off his trip to Hockcliffe and send word he'd been waylaid in London for business. However, it was one thing he'd never done to Mellie: lie to her. And he would not start now.

Nor could he keep himself away from her.

It had taken all his strength to leave her at the end of each Christmastide night to go back to his cold, empty London townhouse and live an entire year before seeing her again.

There was no doubt his cause was a worthy one, but the time away from Hockcliffe had begun to weigh heavily on him.

Seeing Mellie despite her years of deep anguish brought light to Brigham's world.

He longed to love her the way she deserved and show her the affection and love his heart had kept hidden all these years. To prove to her that wedding her hadn't only been an offer to care for her ailing mother and provide a home for the pair; no, his motives that day had been selfish. She'd been in peril, and he'd taken advantage of that by offering for her hand. Could they have grown to love one another without the necessity of the union?

Brigham hadn't the answer to that.

And even in marriage, he feared his love was one-sided and was not to be returned.

"My lord," Peters, his footman, called as he exited the house. "I can take your bag and call for Joseph to come 'round for your horse."

He'd been so preoccupied, he hadn't heard the door open. The shock in the servant's voice at Brigham's unexpected early arrival was warranted. Brigham, and his father before him, had always been timely men, never arriving a moment early nor a moment late.

"Thank you, Peters." He handed his traveling satchel to the servant and started for the front door. Though he only managed a few steps before he halted and turned back toward the footman. "Before we part ways, I have something important in my bag."

He leaned over the satchel, his glasses sliding down his nose, but thankfully, he did not need them to see things up close. Undoing the tie, he rummaged through his hastily folded clothes and books, locating the small, paper-wrapped box.

Melloria's Christmas gift.

A pendant with a long chain, holding the images of her mother and father.

He'd had the necklace commissioned shortly after her mother's death and had meant to journey to Hockcliffe long before Christmastide to give it to her.

He sighed, slipping the box into his coat pocket as he started for the house once more.

He longed to bring a smile to Mellie's face and banish the sorrow that had settled upon her in recent years. He'd witnessed her transformation from a happy, joyous young girl, looking forward to her first London Season, to a woman who was too thin, her shoulders slumped, and her hair hanging limply about her shoulders.

Brigham had been so worried the year before at her crestfallen, sickly appearance he'd sent another London physician to exam her. Thankfully, the man had proclaimed Mellie free of the illness that had robbed her of both her parents.

Even if the pendant brought only a speck of light to her sea-green eyes, it would be worth it.

As he crossed Hockcliffe's threshold, he noticed the silence that lingered. Though a maid could be heard somewhere above stairs, and quiet laughter floated from the kitchens, Brigham was nearly overtaken by the sense of emptiness.

It must be his exhaustion taking over. He needed a bath and sleep before he sought out

Mellie. Instead of heading for the main stairs, he veered toward his study. If he were stalling in making his presence known, he was more the coward than he thought. His study was as quiet as the rest of the house and blessedly vacant.

His desk was as he'd left it the previous year. His shelves housing the same hundreds of books on British law and social reform policies. Even the sideboard stood at the ready with finely crafted glass tumblers and decanters brimming with spirits of every sort.

For the first time in Brigham's life, he wished he were a drinking man.

The conversation to come would be made far easier if he were deep in his cups.

Alas, he was not a man who favored spirit stronger than a dinner sherry.

Only the future would tell if his avoidance of drink continued.

Walking around his large, mahogany desk, he slumped into his chair and laid his head upon the smooth desktop. It was not warm like the neck of his horse, but it was welcome all the same.

Perhaps a few moments' rest and he'd drag himself up to his chambers for a bath and proper attire before going in search of Mellie.

CHAPTER 2

MELLIE PAUSED OUTSIDE the study door to catch her breath. Glancing about the winter-shrouded garden behind her, she marveled at how dissimilar it appeared to the day she and Brigham were wed; no blossoms held tightly to their stems, all the leaves had abandoned their branches to make room for new ones to bud in the spring, and, perhaps the most startling difference, the area's lack of green. It was as if the garden sensed the house was in great mourning.

Her inhales and exhales returned to normal, and she lowered her hood to run her fingers through her knotted hair, made all the more tangled from her mad sprint back to the house.

There was nothing she could do to right her haphazard appearance, however. Not that she'd ever noticed if Brigham took interest in her with regards to her dress and hair.

Mellie listened at the door for a moment but

heard no sounds from inside Brigham's study. She favored the room because she could come and go without the pitying looks or words of condolences from the servants. In this space, she could read, write, or just sit in silence. No one entered the room except to perform the normal weekly dusting and polishing of the wood. In the study, Mellie was not the pitiful, pauper daughter of a baron. She knew the servants only meant to be kind, yet their delicate treatment of her did more to make her feel like a guest in her own home rather than the lady of the manor.

Shaking her head to clear her last thought before tears sprang to her eyes, Mellie pushed the door open on silent hinges and slipped inside, quick to close and latch the door behind her to keep out the winter cold.

With any luck, she'd be able to hurry up to her chambers and have Lilly brush and pin her hair before Brigham sent for her. Perhaps he wouldn't call for her but retire to his own room.

Something had to be amiss, for Brigham had sent word he'd arrive on the morrow.

Mellie turned toward the door as a loud exhale sounded in the room, causing her to jump in fright, her hip hitting the table and scattering the collection of figurines that had been arranged with precise care on top.

Brigham lifted his head from his desk, his glasses askew, and his short curls disheveled. Straightening his glasses, he looked as if he attempted to focus on what had disturbed his slumber.

"My lord," she squeaked, glancing down at the floor and the strewn figurines. "I did not mean to wake you...nor knock your collection from the table." She quickly knelt down and collected the tiny statues, arranging them as best she could.

He remained silent as Mellie stood and turned to face him once more, begging herself to look contrite over her trespassing into his private study, waking him, *and* spilling his figurines to the floor. Thankfully, her clumsiness hadn't resulted in any of Brigham's collection breaking.

To her shock, it wasn't anger or irritation she saw in his expression, nor even frustration at her unexpected distraction.

Mellie stood still before her husband as his stare trailed from her wild, windblown hair to her open cloak that revealed her black gown beneath, to her boot-clad toes then back again, settling somewhere between her bosom and her neck.

Her stomach tightened when she noted his eyes darkening, his lids closing slightly as he gazed up at her from his seated position. If he'd ever looked at her thusly, Mellie did not remember... and it would be very difficult to forget the raw longing in his eyes. Her nipples tightened into hard buds under her coarse shift. If she were not standing before Brigham, she'd dispel with her clothing, as its touch irritated her sensitive skin.

Her chin notched an inch higher. Heat, a pure, scorching warmth pooled between her legs, and her knees quivered.

The slight magnification of his brown eyes behind his spectacles only intensified the desire evident in his eyes. The orbs, normally a deep cocoa hue, now flamed like honey as he continued to stare at her. He pushed back his chair and stood, making her nerves jitter as he refrained from uttering a single word.

Perhaps words are unnecessary, Mellie mused.

The lust in his stare was like a thousand utterances, and each had pulses of pleasure coursing through her. She may be as yet untouched, but Mellie was not ignorant of what transpired between a man and a woman when the door was closed.

Could seducing one's husband be such a simple feat?

Unfortunately, or likely fortunately, they were not in a private chamber but the study. A servant could enter at any moment with a meal or tea for Brigham.

She swallowed, the sound echoing in the quiet room, and she demanded her heart stop racing and her breathing return to normal.

Certainly, he was tired from his travels, hungry for his noonday meal, and looking forward to a few private moments—which Mellie had interrupted.

"I will leave you to some privacy," she mumbled, breaking their stare. "My apologies for interrupting—"

"No." It was spoken quietly, but with a force no amount of volume could match. "Please...stay."

The simple plea had Mellie transfixed. Even if a fire raged around them both, she would be unable to flee the room and Brigham's presence.

CHAPTER 3

HIS FISTS BALLED at his sides as the thickness in his throat threatened to cut off the air his body so desperately needed. All the while, his shame boiled to the surface. He never should have come back to Hockcliffe, at least not in such a wrecked demeanor.

Brigham was helpless to stop the shame, remorse, and scorn that followed.

He was a scoundrel like no other. Mellie stood before him, her mourning attire evident in the black gown nearly hidden under her winter cloak.

She was in pain, swallowed by grief at the recent death of her mother, and all Brigham could ponder was how her soft, wild, strawberry-gold waves would feel against his skin. What glorious curves her gown kept hidden from his view. In his mind, he was stripping the offending fabric from her body.

Unfastening the buttons he knew lay at her back, pulling free her stays, and watching as layer after layer fell to the floor, revealing first her smooth shoulders, then the creamy flesh of her breasts, and next the flare of her womanly hips and long, toned legs. He would remove her stockings one at a time as he knelt before her, pressing his lips to her exposed skin. Certainly, he would not walk away unharmed for the very touch of her would scorch him thoroughly.

If that were the case, Brigham would perish a satisfied man.

He pulled his stare from her, making a show as he removed his glasses and scrubbed at his eyes.

Bloody hell but this was the woman he'd spent countless nights, months, *years* dreaming of.

Here she stood before him, and he could not speak, could not think, could not bring himself to keep his lustful longings within.

Brigham replaced his spectacles, determined to treat Mellie with the respect and reverence she deserved. But when his eyes lit on her once more, Brigham was startled to see not the woman he'd left the previous Christmastide—wary, broken, and her eyes devoid of life—but the lady he'd fallen in love with all those years ago. Her hair had returned to its former luxuriant waves and would certainly shine under the sun that had returned her sallow complexion to a healthy, sun-kissed glow. She stood taller and was no longer reduced to the lanky, rail-thin shell of a woman who spent every ounce of her energy caring for another.

"You have arrived early, my lord."

The melodic note to her voice was that of his

dreams, as well. Yet, there, Mellie never spoke of him as *my lord*. No, it was Brigham, always Brigham—or my love, my dearest, or my everything.

My lord was never what he longed for her to say... not to him. They'd known each other since birth. They'd climbed trees together in their youth; they'd shared a chaste kiss several years later. And now, they were man and wife, even if Brigham had used her grief to bring them to that position.

He swallowed the lump that had settled in his throat and unclenched his fists to run his damp palms down the front of his trousers. "Yes, matters in London concluded earlier than anticipated."

"I do hope all went well." Her gaze had shifted away from him to the stack of papers on his desk.

"It was as fate deemed it to be," he retorted, making no attempt to keep the bitter note from his voice. Odd how fate seemed to have a hand in altering his life at every turn.

"I would not know of such things." Mellie tugged her cloak tighter about her body, blocking his view of her gown beneath, its bodice straining across her bosom and the skirts flowing from her waist to the floor.

However, her words belied the truth. Melloria was quite possibly the most knowledgeable person in the room on the matter of fate. Had fate not stepped into her life, as well, and wreaked havoc? Had fate not altered her course as a London debutante and made her a wife in under two years?

Hell, fate—that evil taskmaster—hadn't so much changed Brigham's course as shortened it. He'd been willing to stand aside and allow

Mellie her time in London, her Season among society; though he'd always known he would offer for her hand. After time in town, surrounded by dashing, honorable men, and beautiful, guileless ladies, Mellie may have chosen to accept his proposal, or she might have turned up her nose at him.

They would never know if they would have chosen one another willingly, had other options been available to them.

Perhaps that's what made it all the more difficult for Brigham to spend time with her when he was at Hockcliffe.

While fate had stepped in and altered their courses, Brigham could have offered her aid without marriage. He could have found a suitable chaperone for Mellie, moved her mother and her to Hockcliffe, and acquired adequate medical treatment—all without tying her to him.

Brigham had been selfish, and continued to be selfish with each passing day.

He'd made certain she was forever bound to him, and then he abandoned her.

Mellie had insisted he remain in London during her mother's final days...and had sent word only after she'd been laid to rest. All the while, Brigham knew he should have been here, should have ignored her pleas for him to remain at his work.

A large portion of him was weak, the truth of the matter lowering his honor. Brigham hadn't had the strength to see Mellie go through the hardship of losing yet another parent. The first time had nearly killed him.

And now here they were, together once more. Though she stood so still, he'd almost forgotten she was in the room, not just a vision he'd conjured.

Brigham moved from behind his desk, his Hessians weighing down his feet as he stopped before her.

There was nearly a foot separating them. Brigham didn't trust himself to move even a fraction of an inch closer to her, though he could feel her warmth. Her chin tilted up slightly, and she met his stare once more, her green eyes softening.

Could it be that she sensed the struggle he faced? Had word reached her about his failed bill in London? Did she seek to comfort him when it was she who needed *his* strength?

Brigham longed to reach out to her. Desired her in his arms. Wanted nothing more than a brief moment with her as they'd had in their youth. No distractions, unburdened by the present, and free of obligations.

Thus far, he was unworthy of even so much as touching Mellie.

"I think it best I retire to my chambers," he scoffed, taking a step back from her. "I am filthy and wrinkled from travel, and in need of time to freshen up before our evening meal."

She gave him a slight nod.

With a curt bow, Brigham fled his study.

He didn't pause to glance over his shoulder. He did not slow down when he reached the main stairs. He did not so much as acknowledge Mellie's lady's maid when he passed her in the upstairs hall.

No, Brigham did not stop until he was safely in the confines of his private chambers. The sound of the door closing echoed loudly down the hall as he shut himself inside and threw the latch into place. Leaning against the door, he closed his eyes and allowed himself a moment to collect his thoughts—and suppress the urge to return downstairs, pull Mellie into his arms, and kiss her as he'd longed to do since their wedding day.

Sometime later—it could have been a few minutes or several hours—he heard footsteps in the hall outside his door. But, quickly, they retreated, and the only other door in the corridor opened and closed as Mellie no doubt entered her own chambers.

CHAPTER 4

MELLIE STARED AT her image in the looking glass, truly seeing herself for the first time in ages. The full-length mirror had always been in her chambers, but in recent years, Mellie barely noted her appearance. It was far more common that she turned down her maid's assistance when dressing or pinning her hair. The state of her appearance hadn't mattered, for it was her mother's care and comfort Mellie applied herself to day in and day out…not the cut of her gown or the quality of her slippers, or even the stylish flare of her curls.

Who would have been near to notice anyways?

But things had changed since the previous day, had they not?

A light tap sounded at her door. "Enter."

As she watched in the mirror, Lilly closed the door behind her and hurried to Mellie's dressing table. "Can I pin your hair, my lady?"

For the span of a moment, Mellie wondered

if it mattered if her curly locks were pinned atop her head, bound at her neck, or sheared off. Brigham had sent his regrets the night before, calling off on their meal due to his exhaustion, and so Mellie had had a plate delivered to his room as she dined alone in the hall. Not the way she'd envisioned spending her evening; however, it had given her much time to think.

"Allow me to tie my sash, and then I think I would like my hair down, mayhap pinned behind one ear?"

The glow of Lilly's excitement beamed, illuminating the already sunlit room. "Very good, my lady."

Could it be that Mellie was not the only one brightened by Brigham's arrival? She'd noted a positively lighthearted air in the house during her evening meal. Cook had even taken her guidance and prepared shepherd's pie, Brigham's favorite.

Mellie moved slowly to her dressing cabinet, the doors already thrown wide from when she'd searched for the perfect gown—among her six options. She'd never been one for finery in excess or even vanity for that matter. Her cabinet held only what she needed: several gowns, two pairs of slippers, one pair of half boots, and underpinnings. A few ribbons were nestled in a tiny shell Brigham had brought her from Sheerness in Kent for their first Christmastide as husband and wife. She possessed no jewelry beyond the plain gold band he'd given her on their wedding day.

Quickly riffling through her stockings and such, Mellie had a moment's hesitation as she pulled out a long, midnight blue silk sash. The material was smooth and cool against her fingertips. So far, Mellie hadn't strayed from blacks and greys during her time of mourning—but she suspected this day was important. This day, she would take great care in her attire and appearance, if for nothing but to gain Brigham's attention.

Her husband's stay at Hockcliffe would not last longer than a day or two, at most.

Lilly stepped forward, taking the silk sash from Mellie and wrapping it about the high waist of her gown before tying it at her back.

"It is lovely," her maid sighed. "But it will be all the more attractive when I am done with your hair."

Attractive?

Mellie had never seen herself as striking in any way. Certainly, she had the classic appearance of an English rose, though her hair had always held a bit too much red for her liking, her skin had turned pale and sickly over the last several years, and it was only recently that she noted her gowns no longer hung limply from her thin frame.

She took a seat at her dressing table, and Lilly went to work with her brush and pins.

Turning her face slightly, Mellie scrutinized her reflection. Perhaps there had been a time when she'd thought herself pretty, or at least comely enough by Hertfordshire standards. If she lifted her chin at just the right angle, her neck appeared nearly swanlike, her petite ears tucked under her hair, and her large almond-shaped eyes sparkled.

"Should I change my gown?" she mused. "Perchance I have something with a—"

Mellie's voice cut off as she met Lilly's knowing stare in the mirror.

She was going to say *low-cut neckline*.

"Oh, do not look at me thusly, Lilly," Mellie chided, in hopes of distracting her maid. "And do hurry, or I will be late for breakfast."

"Breakfast with Lord Whitmore?" the girl prodded.

"Do you mean my husband?" Mellie corrected, narrowing her stare on the servant. "Because, yes, with Lord Whitmore. That is what wedded couples do when in residence with one another—they dine… together."

Mellie held Lilly's stare, refusing to be the first to look away, mainly because she wasn't sure if the words were meant for Lilly or to reassure herself that dining together was, in fact, what wedded couples did. Heavens, there was a great possibility Brigham would request his meal in his room, as had been the case the night before.

And she would be made to dine alone…again.

Poppycock. If Mellie sought to tempt her husband, she would actually need time in his presence. Her gown and hair would not matter a whit if he never laid eyes on her.

"Done, my lady." Lilly stepped back and clasped her hands at her throat. "You are beautiful."

"I appear adequately gowned and coiffed for a morning meal," Mellie corrected, but she couldn't take her eyes off the woman staring back at her. Her hair was pinned behind one ear but hung free down her back and over the opposite shoulder, highlighting her tanned skin. She'd spent much time outdoors in recent months, and her complexion was the better for it. "Thank you, Lilly."

Mellie stood from the bench, careful not to

muss her hair as she smoothed the wrinkles from her skirts.

It was time to tempt her husband.

She only prayed he was below and not cloistered in his room.

"Enjoy your meal, my lady. I will have your cloak brought down to the hall for your morning walk."

She smiled at Lilly. The maid was skilled at her post and had provided Mellie with a listening ear on more occasions than could be counted on two hands.

"Again, thank you," Mellie said and hurried from the room to the main stairs.

She took hold of her skirts as she descended to the foyer.

A cold draft hit her squarely in the face when Mr. Danvers, the Whitmore butler, closed the front door.

"Good morn, my lady," he greeted with his usual cheerful tone. "Shall I have Cook bring your meal to the dining hall?"

Mellie glanced over his shoulder at the front door, but try as she might, she could not see through the thick wooden panel. Someone had recently left, but who departed the house at this ungodly hour? And where could they be going? Even the market in town was an hour from opening.

"My lady?"

Shaking her head, she smiled at Danvers. "If that is where Lord Whitmore is pleased to dine, yes."

"My lord has broken his fast and left."

Left? Her skin prickled at the word. Could Brigham have departed for London so quickly? Certainly, he had no pressing matters to attend to on Christmastide Eve morn.

"Where, may I ask, has he gone?"

"He went to the steward's cottage."

"But Mr. Briars is away to visit family for the holiday," Mellie countered.

"I told Lord Whitmore as much, but he thought the time good to look over the ledgers for the year."

Mellie pursed her lips to keep from snapping at the butler. If Brigham were avoiding her, it was between her and her husband, not the servants. Though she could not tamp down her ire. Certainly, there was time after the holiday for business matters.

There was no time to contemplate why Brigham's early rising and departure irritated her so much.

"I will make certain he knows Mr. Briars is away," Mellie said, turning toward the stairs. If she were going outdoors, she was not senseless enough to brave the elements without her cloak. And true to form, Lilly made her way down the hall from the servant's stairs with Mellie's long, black wrap in hand. "I will not be long," she called to the butler as she slipped her arms into the waiting garment. "I will break my fast when I return from the steward's cottage."

"Shall I have a horse brought round?"

"No, it is only a brisk walk away." Mellie waved off the servant, thankful for his concern, but she was in a rush to set off after Brigham.

If she didn't catch him at the steward's office, it was likely he'd find yet another task that needed his attention which would keep him from the main house.

It would be harder than that to avoid Mellie.

She had plans, and they had naught to do with poring over old ledgers in the dusty steward's cottage—and everything to do with capturing Brigham's notice.

Mellie only hoped she knew what to do with his attention once she had it.

CHAPTER 5

BRIGHAM ADJUSTED HIS position in the rickety chair his estate steward, Briars, used when maintaining the ledgers for Hockcliffe. The seat was too hard, the back too straight, and the location too far from Mellie. But again, he'd spent the last five years keeping his distance from her...a simple few minute's ride by horse was far closer than London—or the wilds of Scotland. He glanced at the empty hearth, debating the merits of starting a fire to ward off the early morning chill. There was no doubt he'd be at the steward's office for some time as he was finding it difficult to rein in his thoughts long enough to study the accounts.

There was something else...*someone* else he'd much prefer to study.

Instead, he was in Briars' office, and Mellie was likely still abed, gaining her final hour of restful sleep.

Tenant dues. Crop rotation schedules. Staff allowances. Kitchen receipts from the market.

It was all a haze. Turning another page in the accounting ledger for the crop sharing land nearest the village, Brigham attempted to concentrate on the columns neatly scripted on the paper.

Corn was in high demand, while wheat and barley had seen a decrease since last winter. The oat crop had suffered a major catastrophe when an unidentified insect contaminated the fields closest to the manor. The livestock had been kept clear of the land and moved to the east for grazing before being herded inland toward Oxford and away from the coastal breezes that still managed to make their way to Hertfordshire.

Briars was a shrewd asset to Hockcliffe Manor and the Whitmore family as a whole. His detailed accounting made it possible for Brigham to surmise how his estate was doing in just a glance. For many years, that was all the time Brigham could allot to the scrutiny of his ledgers.

However, if Brigham were to make a smooth transition to his country seat, he must needs better educate himself in the ways of his property.

It was no different than collecting data, compiling research, and proposing a reform bill.

He only need apply himself to the task at hand.

Yet his thoughts continued to return to another task that was much overdue and should demand his attention over all else.

Mellie.

Her happiness. Her comfort. Her well-being in every form.

It had taken every ounce of strength he possessed to keep from seeking her out the night before—at her meal or later in her private chambers. He was up at first light, prowling the hall in hopes she'd exit, and he could gain another view of her splendid beauty.

She hadn't left her room...and Brigham knew, for the time being, it was for the best. Until he could gain a firm hold of his longings, it was not advisable for him to allow his emotions to overtake his good sense. There was much he owed the woman and lusting after her like a randy London dandy fresh from University was not one of them.

He leaned back in his chair and massaged his temples, though the light pressure gave no relief to his aching head.

They need speak of the grave matters between them; namely, Brigham's need to cast himself at her feet and beg her forgiveness before anything could develop anew. Be it a renewed friendship or the resurgence of the closeness they once shared, he would not hedge his hopes on either. It was just as likely she'd grown accustomed to her life of solitude and wished naught for his presence at Hockcliffe.

He need remember the folly of misplaced confidence. Had he not learned a severe lesson over the last several weeks?

The fact that he'd come face-to-face with the woman he'd once known was what had thrown him off course, given him pause, and incited a long dormant lust he hadn't known still burned so strongly within him.

Brigham glanced at the windowpane next to the door of the cottage as the sun rose ever higher in the sky. No matter how much time he spent away from Hertfordshire, he never grew accustomed to any other sunrise. Something—or someone—kept his heart at Hockcliffe. His time at University had been no different, as he'd counted the days, the hours until he was free to journey home. Was it the place or Melloria who tethered him to this land?

If she'd agreed to accompany him to London after they wed, would the need to return here still be as strong within him?

It was said that home was where the heart lay, but Brigham could not understand the bonds linking him to a woman who did not know she held his heart. And he would not delude himself into thinking her heart was meant for him.

He would not question his decision.

Pushing back his chair, Brigham strode to the hearth and stared into its sooty, cavernous cove. Hockcliffe was where he belonged, where he should have remained, and where he needed to be to find his future. So many years had been squandered chasing after dreams and aspirations that, while vitally imperative to England's future, shouldn't have overshadowed his duties at home: to his wife, his servants, and his land.

Worse yet, it was only now, in the aftermath of his failure, that he realized Mellie was more important than any calling in London. In the blink of an eye, everything in town had been stripped from him—it had all disappeared—and he was left with only one thing... Mellie.

With shaking, unsteady hands, Brigham piled the logs high in the hearth and spread the small twigs and sticks at the base before turning to collect the flint from its place. As he struck the metals together, a sense of rightness filled him. Using his hands to produce something as basic as a fire for warmth had his confidence increasing.

He could do this. He could admit his failures, confess his betrayal, and beg for Mellie's forgiveness.

The time was upon him and certainly long overdue.

He owed her the option to cast him from Hockcliffe—as was her right.

Returning to his seat, he lowered down with a heavy sigh.

After stating his piece, Brigham had to be man enough to accept whatever dictate Mellie set forth.

Her mercy was something he was uncertain he was worthy of.

Perhaps a few more hours away from the manor would strengthen his resolve, and he'd find the right words to tell her all while keeping his longing for her from spilling forth and further muddling their precarious situation.

He was hiding...and he damn well bloody knew it.

The question was, what was he willing to do about it?

MELLIE WATCHED BRIGHAM through the thick grime on the window as he rubbed his temples, knelt to start a fire, and then sat lax in his chair. He was an academic man, a lord more accustomed to the darkened halls of Parliament than the stalls at Tattersalls, yet that did not diminish his presence. He did not appear any less broad of shoulder or tan of skin than the servants who worked the fields around Hockcliffe. Perhaps Brigham had taken up fencing or bare-knuckle boxing while in town to hone his physique and remain active.

Closing her eyes, she envisioned him, not in the full garb of a fencer, but bare-chested with his hands wrapped in cloth, and short pants to enable easy, swift movements—his hands raised in defense as he danced around the boxing area, keeping space between him and his opponent.

A sound from within had her lids snapping open once more to see Brigham standing again and pacing before the hearth, his hands shoved deeply into the pockets of the coat he had yet to remove.

Something was amiss with him, Mellie was certain of it.

Never had he arrived at Hockcliffe with such a dark cloud looming over him, his shoulders caving in, and dark shadows under his eyes, indicating he hadn't slept well for some time. His usual carefree manner and jovial nature was lacking, as well, and never had he outright avoided her presence when in residence. It was a fact that they'd never shared a marriage bed, but Brigham hadn't ever called off on a meal with her or evaded her company.

Whatever weighed on him was great enough that he did not seek to burden Mellie with it. What the man did not realize was that his avoidance made it all the more important to her to discover what had him so crestfallen...and repair it.

In any way she could.

Yet, Mellie was at a loss for how to discover anything if he continually sought to evade her.

But she had her own plans for his short stay at Hockcliffe.

Perhaps it was possible to combine those two goals: help banish his melancholy mood and repay his kindness.

She'd lived for so many years under a black cloud of grief, and Mellie did not want that for Brigham. All she needed was time to reconnect with him, and she could certainly restore his happiness.

The last several months, with no ailing mother to keep her occupied, had opened her eyes to many things—namely, hope for her future. She'd been blessed with a kind, compassionate husband who had done everything in his power to help Mellie and keep her mother comfortable during her last years. It was time Mellie was there for her spouse.

On the morrow, Christmastide morning would dawn, and Brigham would likely speak of his intentions to depart Hockcliffe.

Her future—and his—hinged on the present.

Not tomorrow, not a fortnight from now, and certainly not a year from now when once again Brigham returned for his short holiday stay.

Mellie glanced down at her tightly bound cloak and hastily unbuttoned it until her midnight blue sash was visible beneath. A quick touch at her ear confirmed that her hair was as it should be, pinned at one side and hanging freely down her back. Her cheeks were already rosy from the harsh December cold.

She lifted her chin and grasped the latch on the door; the freezing metal could be felt even through her gloves. A part of her shouted to withdraw her hand and return to the manor, await Brigham therein. But another—much louder—part of her, willed her to push open the door.

And greet her husband as if they both belonged at the steward's office.

An overpowering heat gathered at the apex of her thighs, and her breasts swelled, pulling the material of her gown tight across her chest.

Something about the entire situation was intoxicating, and her mind swam as if she'd overindulged in dinner sherry.

As soon as she entered the cottage and closed the door solidly behind her, she and Brigham would be alone, without a soul to interrupt them.

Her brow furrowed. This was possibly the first time since they were young children gallivanting between Hockcliffe and Tapton property that they would be unequivocally alone. Even at Hockcliffe there were always servants close at hand, and Brigham's sister and her family normally arrived with Brigham from London.

They'd shared sparse few moments in his study the day before, but they hadn't been truly unaccompanied there either.

But here, in this cottage, they had no fear of a servant stumbling upon them.

Smiling brightly to hide her own nerves, Mellie pushed the door open and greeted Brigham. He no longer paced the room but sat behind the modest desk. "Good morning, my lord."

His eyes narrowed behind his rounded glasses before widening. "Mellie?" He swallowed hard before continuing, leaning forward in his seat. "Ah, what brings you all the way out here? It is dreadfully cold outside."

"I walk most mornings and noticed someone was here." There was little reason to confess that she'd followed him to the cottage, when in fact, her daily walks did take her by the steward's residence on most days. "When I saw your horse tied outside, I figured I should stop and inquire if you were in need of anything."

Their eyes remained locked when Mellie

pushed the door closed at her back and stepped farther into the room, which suddenly seemed smaller due to her presence—and his. Neither so much as breathed. Mellie stifled her breath for fear she'd startle him from his silence, and he'd send her back to the manor. But as for Brigham, she was uncertain what kept him frozen before her. He did not stand to greet her nor allow his eyes to release her stare.

Mellie was not versed in matters of the flesh; indeed, she'd never even so much as discussed the topic with anyone. The hard stare locked on hers proclaimed she was to learn today—this very moment if Mellie had any say in the matter. Brigham, the man she'd adored in her youth whom had given her everything in her adulthood, was the only one she trusted wholeheartedly. He would not lead her astray nor cause her any harm.

"Thank you for your concern and thoughtfulness, but I am merely studying the ledgers"—he tapped his finger on the open book—"before Briars returns from holiday."

Brigham's head dropped, and he focused on the tome before him once more...however, he didn't demand she leave.

And so, she slipped her arms from her cloak and deposited it on the chair across from the steward's desk and then proceeded to remove her black gloves, one finger at a time until her hands were bare. She set the accessories on the chair beside her discarded overgarment.

Not once did Brigham glance up from his work, though the stiffening of his back indicated he was acutely aware of Mellie's presence. To test her newfound power, she paced slowly around the desk he sat behind until she was at his back.

"Do allow me to assist you in your examination." She leaned in close, certain her breath caressed his neck. "I have often wondered what kept the steward so busy nearly all year round."

"Yes, busy man—much to do—"

Mellie placed her hands on Brigham's shoulders, once more surprised at their broad width, as he tensed beneath her touch.

For a moment, she kept her fingers still, begged her hands to apply no pressure to him for fear he'd push her away, but when he remained silent and still for several minutes, Mellie gently kneaded his stiff shoulders. Her heart beat erratically within her chest, her nipples hardening more than before as the material of her shift agitated the tender buds.

His entire body shuddered under her fingers.

Her breath hitched, and she leaned ever closer as his heady male scent surrounded her. It was a tempting mix of the stables from his ride here and something far earthier, as if he'd spent time in the woods. She knew this to be impossible, for he'd departed the manor and rode straight to the cottage, so she figured it must be a scent unique to him alone.

Instead of relaxing under the gentle pressure of her hands, his shoulders only became more rigid, and his head lifted from his work to stare out the far window.

The cords of his muscles flexed under her hold, causing a tingle to course down her spine, and her knees to weaken.

Why had they waited so long for this moment?

Her arousal at their mere touch was nearly

enough to send her crashing to her knees. For her to beg him to remove his coat and unfasten the long row of buttons down her back.

Mellie remained silent, allowing her hands to wander from his shoulders to his upper arms, the cut of his jacket straining over his biceps. She wondered what other surprises he kept hidden under his proper attire.

Her cheeks flushed at the thought, but she refused to back down.

Glancing over his shoulder, Mellie saw that his eyes had drifted shut, his lips pressed tightly into a firm line.

Was it possible he did not welcome her advances?

CHAPTER 6

ALARM BELLS—NO, ear-piercing sirens!—went off in Brigham's head.

This was not how things were supposed to progress. Mellie was not to be at the steward's cottage. She was not meant to remove her cloak and her—*gulp*—gloves. And she, most definitely, positively, unquestionably was not destined to place her bare, naked hands upon him in such an intimate manner.

Naked… His mind spiraled to more than just her hands being bared before him.

Oh, dear blessed Father above.

Brigham was losing the thin thread of composure he'd held on to since her arrival in the doorway.

Her breath was like a warm summer breeze on his neck. She was so close, a lock of her long, reddish blonde hair fell upon his shoulder. Blast it all, but he had to halt himself from reaching up and bringing it to his nose. Would she smell of strawberries? Vanilla? Perhaps she'd have the scent of blueblossoms clinging to her as she had on their wedding day.

He pinched the bridge of his nose, concentrating on why he was at the steward's cottage in the first place.

Yes, he remembered. His mind was foggy with lust, but he did, indeed, remember his purpose herein.

He'd come in search of a private space where he did not have to fear interruption for the specific purpose of thinking through all he was to say to Mellie when next they met. He'd thought to outline a conversation where he would confess his misdeeds and beg her forgiveness, then and only then, would they speak of the past and decide, as rational adults, if they had a future together or if their time to be a true wedded couple had come and gone while both were preoccupied with other things. Certainly, Mellie's ailing mother had been far more important than their marriage, though Brigham knew his work in London hadn't been imperative enough to keep him from his husbandly responsibilities.

Bloody hell. He never should have abandoned her for his lofty aspirations among the *ton*. It had taken him five long years for this truth to break through his thick head.

…and now it could be too late.

What had they been speaking of before she placed her hands on his shoulders?

Mr. Briars, his steward.

For some reason, speaking of the servant in this moment—as Mellie's hands moved from his upper arms, back to his shoulders, and down toward his chest—did not seem a wise choice.

Or even a discussion Brigham capable of.

He exhaled, his breath leaving him in more of a moan than a sigh as his eyes drifted closed.

They were alone and over a mile from Hockcliffe manor and two miles from town. No one was close enough to give this private moment an ounce of propriety. But then again, he and Mellie were husband and wife and were not in need of a chaperone.

Her hands drifted lower still, nearly reaching his stomach as they glided over his jacket.

"You are very tense, my lord." With his eyes still closed, he could feel her lips by his ear.

"Brig-ham," he hissed and immediately sucked in his breath as something grazed his neck, directly behind his ear.

"Yes." The single word quaked on her lips. "Brigham.

At his name on her lips and her closeness apparent, his manhood stiffened and became so rigid he fairly ached with agony.

He'd sought out this cottage to gain some distance from her, not be confronted by his own lack of restraint when it came to his wife.

Brigham leapt from his seat, his action causing Mellie to take a step back as he sidestepped the chair and turned to face her. Her hands were still held in midair, and her face paled with fright before color blossomed in her cheeks.

He'd wanted to speak with her, not cause her embarrassment or fright.

Reaching forward, he took her hand in both of his, marveling at how small it was nestled in his. How warm her skin was. How smooth her fingers were.

Suddenly, she was against him, yet he hadn't moved. The straining bulge in his trousers pressed insistently to her belly.

Mellie had been the one to close the distance between them.

He was all hard contours to her soft curves.

There was no chance of Brigham hiding his arousal from her, and the knowing look in her green eyes told him she knew exactly what he was thinking.

"My apologies, Mellie," he whispered low. "I have been under immense strain lately and my body—it is not—"

She pulled her hand from his grasp, and Brigham feared he'd insulted her, caused her humiliation no woman should experience at the hands of her husband, yet she did not step away nor flee the cottage.

Instead, she lifted her arms and wrapped them around his neck...and pulled his lips to hers.

It was heaven, yet burned like hellfire.

It was Brigham's salvation, but would surely result in his being thrown into purgatory.

This was what he'd been longing for all these years; however, never did he delude himself into thinking he deserved it.

Melloria, his first and only love, pressed close; their mouths locked together as each struggled to hold on.

Her ripe mouth anchored them together as she pressed her body to his, claiming him as hers. Though Brigham had always known he belonged to her and only her. Her lips were lush and sweet, and he wrapped his arms about her waist to keep their mouths locked. As if sensing his heightened arousal, she ran her fingers up his neck and tangled them in his curling hair, holding his face to hers.

Her tight grasp on him was unnecessary, as

he had no urge to let her go, no desire to allow her to slip away from him.

Tentatively, Brigham's hands moved lower until they cupped her bottom, and he gently kneaded her rounded derriere gently as they deepened their kiss.

He wanted this moment to last forever—if only to delay the inevitable.

To avoid having to confess his failures in London and his regrets about having abandoned her all these years. His remorse for being gone when her mother passed away. And the heart of the matter, that he was too foolish to realize the import of it all until after everything he'd worked so hard for had been crushed. All these years he'd spent countless hours away from home. And when he was in residence at Hockcliffe, he'd droned on and on about his reform bills, the important men he'd met with, and the topics of discussion labored over during their meetings. All things that had been significant to Brigham, while Mellie suffered neglect at the hands of her estranged husband.

In response to his wayward thoughts, Brigham pulled her closer still, his knees touching hers through layers and layers of skirting and underpinnings, yet urging her thighs to spread. Oh, how he fought the impulse to dispel with the material that separated them, that kept his eyes and hands from the rounded flare of her hips and her from touching the corded muscle of his chest and shoulders.

They'd been wedded for years, but Brigham had never tasted the nape of her neck, never allowed his fingers to trail up her bare legs, and certainly never thought he'd ever have the right to have his lips upon hers.

Only in his dreams did he touch her like

this—with reverence, adoration, and awe.

Brigham breathed deeply through his nose so as not to displace their mouths, yet the action served only to fill his entire being with her scent. So uniquely Mellie.

Not that of a berry or vanilla or even blueblossoms. No, the scent that clung to her was as if every flower, every blossom, every sweetness came together just for her; to blend as one to make her extraordinary fragrance. It was not something carried by any local mercantile, nor the creation of the esteemed Floris of London. Certainly, if he could bottle Mellie's essence and sell the concoction, they would never see a day without immense wealth.

Brigham scoffed, breaking his lips from hers. He would never, ever allow another to get close enough to bask in her fragrance.

She was his. Had always been meant for him. Surely, he'd been created specifically to love and cherish her. The way their bodies melded together now was evidence of that fact.

They both panted hard as Brigham looked down into the green eyes that'd haunted his nights since before he recognized their connection. But what did he see therein?

CHAPTER 7

MELLIE COULD NOT remove her stare from Brigham. He was everything she'd always wanted. He alone was the one man who could provide her with protection, security, comfort—and, dare she dream… love. However, even in this moment, she sensed him retreating into his proper, gentlemanly shell. The mask he always wore in her presence.

He could not hide his desire for her. His need was evident. There was no masking the throbbing manhood in his trousers or the scorching arousal apparent in his intense stare.

The time gifted to them did not allow for games or distractions. She would not stand by while Brigham sidestepped her and denied them both what they so evidently needed.

Tightening her arms around his neck once more, Mellie brought his lips to hers as she pushed to her tiptoes. Besides a chaste kiss in their youth, she'd never kissed another—and she certainly enjoyed kissing Brigham, as well as the power she felt as he melted in her arms during their embrace.

For once, she was taking the lead in their relationship. She was in control, and she dictated when, where, and how far this intimacy went.

She was a vixen, a siren, utterly wanton…and Mellie didn't care a whit.

Brigham's touch did this to her. It was as hot as the blaze in the hearth and thawed the frozen bits of her heart.

With their mouths pressed close once more, Mellie parted her lips, and immediately, his tongue shot forward, exploring and tangling with hers as, all the while, she nestled her body closer to his. But his hands no longer remained on her backside, caressing and massaging her trembling flesh. Instead, with aching slowness, he moved his palms to her waist and slid his light touch up her sides to the curve of her heaving bosom. Despite her many layers of clothing, Mellie felt his fingers as they journeyed upward—felt the heat of his touch.

She sighed into his mouth as he reached behind her and popped her buttons from their holds—one at a time with swift fingers. Never once did he pull his lips from hers, and never once did the rhythm of their kiss veer off course.

Blessedly, her bodice loosened, giving Mellie the opportunity to breathe in deeply. When her chest expanded, her breasts pushed more firmly against his chest, fighting for space as Brigham took not even a step away from her.

The warm air provided by the hearth washed over her now bare skin at her shoulders.

She pulled back a mere inch. "Brigham?"

Mellie was uncertain what question she asked: that he stop and allow her a moment to breathe, or speed up and ravish her with all due haste.

Brigham trailed light kisses across her cheek and down her neck, nipping along the way.

She had no desire for him to stop, but she was also hesitant to increase their tempo. Instead, Brigham made the decision for her and slowed their pace as his lips moved farther down and over her clavicle to her mounded cleavage. All the while, his hand tugged at the shoulder of her gown, exposing more of her heated skin to his touch.

There was nothing for her to do but throw her head back and revel in his caresses, concentrate on his every touch, and pray to the Lord above that her knees did not buckle beneath her.

Brigham trailed his lips along her shoulder and down her arm as he inched the bodice of her gown ever lower. It was his turn to torture her as his breath stroked the globes of her heavy breasts—sweet, sweet agony.

Her eyes sprang open, and her entire body tensed as his lips gently grazed her budded nipple.

A shiver threatened to have her collapsing before him as wave after wave of pure, raw, pleasure coursed through her and pooled between her clenched thighs.

Was this what women hurried to their wedded bed for each night?

A part of her screamed that there was more to come, far more pleasure to be had.

This was what she'd longed to give Brigham. The only gift that was hers to give, as it were. Her. And, if she were blessed, a Whitmore heir.

As it was, they would both reap much happiness and pleasure from their union.

An uninhibited moan escaped her when Brigham latched on to her nipple and gently suckled through the fabric of her bodice, his hand delicately kneading her still-covered breast.

She tilted to the side, her legs finally giving in to the pleasure, but Brigham was there to hold her upright as his lips began their journey back up, over her mounded breast, to her neck. The air in the room brushed her sensitive, hardened peak and a pant caught in her throat.

The urge to push him back down toward her bust, demand he apply his skills ever more to her as yet still bodice and shift-covered breast, was nearly more than she could suppress as she sucked in a ragged breath.

"Yes, this…this…" She could barely force the words past her kiss-swollen lips. "Brigham, I—"

"Shhh," he whispered at her throat. "I know what you want."

How could he know what she wanted when Mellie hadn't any idea?

But his kisses and scorching touch continued. This was the way of things between them: they spoke of trivial things to mask what they truly had need to discuss. And now, he plied her with pleasure beyond her wildest dreams, making speech unimportant.

There was so much Mellie longed to tell Brigham, though… before it was too late.

If they had only this brief, intimate moment she wanted him to know that she gave herself freely and with no reservations.

"Brigham." Her voice cracked, but she pushed on. "I have been so blessed by your kindness. I seek to give you the heir you deserve." Mellie paused, pulling air into her lungs as his hand stilled at her breast. "This is the only gift I have to give, to repay you for all you've done for me."

He pulled his mouth from her cheek, and his hands dropped to his sides.

"Brigham?" Mellie took a step toward him, seeking to bring him back to her, but he moved away as his head fell to his hands—hands that had only a moment before been giving her immense pleasure.

"This is about an heir?" he demanded in a low, calm voice.

"Yes, but I—"

"You think I came to Hockcliffe in want of an heir?" He pivoted away from her and retrieved his glasses from the table, jamming them on his face with more force than necessary. "You think my only motivation in coming here was to bed you?"

Mellie's mind reeled at his sudden anger as she attempted to wrap her mind around what was transpiring between them. "Does not every lord seek an heir?"

"No lord is foolish enough to believe they can beget an heir without a proper marriage first."

But they were properly wed, were they not?

"I did not come here to bed you, Melloria."

A treacherous sob broke free from her lips as she covered her flaming face with her hands.

She'd known all along this could very well be the outcome. Years had passed since they wed, and never once had either of them sought comfort or pleasure in the arms of the other. It could only mean that Brigham had searched for those things with another outside their marriage. She could not, would never, blame him for finding love and affection elsewhere.

Brigham was a man with needs; needs Mellie

had been unable to fulfill either physically or emotionally.

Was there another woman he sought to birth his child?

Without another glance at Brigham, she turned and fled the cottage, leaving the door open in her wake—escaping into the icy cold December morning, her cloak and gloves forgotten, her attire in disarray.

Mellie hadn't a direction in mind, nor was she capable of such focus as she ran through the biting wind, its frigid tendrils lashing at her face and exposed skin. Clumsily, she kept moving as she pulled up her gown to cover her, but clasping the buttons at her back proved impossible as she stumbled over the hem of her dress.

Righting herself, she sped on, never glancing behind her.

For what would injure her more: his initial rejection and horror at her words, or that he didn't chase after her?

CHAPTER 8

BRIGHAM PACED BACK and forth in the tiny cottage office, unable to bring himself to return to rational thought. He removed his spectacles and tossed them onto the desk, but they skidded and fell off the side, clattering to the plank floor. He didn't retrieve them, he did not even hurry over to see if he'd damaged them...blast it all, but he had no desire to even look at them.

Much as he was doing now with Mellie. He should have run after her. Should have hurried to her and made certain she was uninjured despite his harsh, cruel words. He should want to behold nothing but her.

She was selfless to a fault.

...and he'd failed her once again.

Peddling her body to *give* him an heir? She deserved far more than to be reduced to a breeding tool as a way to serve both Brigham and society, producing a much coveted and demanded heir. She was worth far more than what her body could produce. Using her for that purpose would be the ultimate betrayal, something beyond forgiveness, no matter how profusely he begged at her feet.

And that was exactly where Brigham deserved to be: at Mellie's feet, begging her for mercy he didn't deserve and hadn't earned.

First, he'd convinced her to wed him when she was grieving her dead father.

Then he'd abandoned her to her own hell, leaving her to care for her dying mother.

And lastly, he'd only returned but once a year, sharing nothing of himself. In turn, she'd kept her longings and desires to herself. He'd been rash to think she'd ever open up to him when he'd done nothing but keep her at arm's length.

He shouldn't have come to Hockcliffe. He should have accepted her choice to remain in the country unburdened by him.

To think Mellie thought *she* owed him something—anything.

It was Brigham who owed her everything.

He hadn't been man enough to stick by her side after they wed, help her care for her mother, and discover if there could be true affection between them. They'd kissed once. They'd spent nearly every holiday together, their families being very close. They'd played, they'd laughed, they'd conversed together for all these years. Since childhood, they'd spoken of grave matters and trivial occurrences; however, that had all stopped when they wed. But why?

Brigham had long held that they had, indeed, shared a mutual affection in their youth.

He scrubbed at his face, running his hands through his tangled curls. That was a bad choice, too, as all he could think of was Mellie's delicate fingers caressing his neck and tugging at his hair when they were wrapped in their intimate embrace.

Why had he sought his own work, leaving their budding love to deteriorate?

Love.

Neither had ever so much as spoken the word before or after they wed. Brigham because it would have crushed him, left him without drive to go on if she did not return his love.

Nevertheless, Brigham had loved her. Continued to love her, if only from a distance.

How had they never found time to discuss this?

His heavy steps echoed angrily in the tiny cottage, mirroring the disdain he felt for himself.

"A gentleman?" he snorted. "Hardly."

What sort of man worth anything allowed his wife to wallow and languish alone in the country for years on end?

A coward.

And he'd thought he could return home with a trinket for Christmastide and all would be as it should have been years ago. Perhaps he'd lost all sense with his failure in London.

London.

He'd had plans before her father fell ill. Mellie was to journey to town during her seventeenth year for a proper London Season. Brigham would have followed behind her, watching as she explored life among society while he championed his first reform bill. They would have eventually come together, and he'd thought to offer for her hand before the Season was complete.

Instead, the sickness—which took so many hardworking coalminers—had struck, bringing her father low long before his time. Mellie had selflessly delayed her Season, unknowingly dooming herself to nearly eight years of hardship.

What would have happened if fate hadn't dealt them the harsh blow it had and made their marriage a necessity?

Would Mellie have chosen another man to wed, perchance a far more suitable lord? A man whose courage and honor dwarfed Brigham's?

She deserved a man unafraid to speak of love—a man who didn't find it necessary to hide his true feelings their entire lives.

His cowardly way of securing their marriage had denied Mellie the husband—and no doubt the horde of children—she'd been destined to have. It was a regret he would live with his entire life and be haunted by in the hereafter.

There was no one and nothing to blame but himself.

Pivoting once more and heading back toward the desk, Brigham noted something lying upon the chair. He swooped down and retrieved his glasses. He set them to rights and brought the object into focus.

Mellie's cloak and gloves.

She'd fled the cottage, into the icy morning, without the benefit of cloak or gloves—and with her gown askew. It was a long, brisk walk back to the manor, especially in the harsh December weather. Even with the snow holding off for the better part of the season, the biting winds would make their way through her gown and chill her to the bone within minutes. She'd be near freezing long before she made it back to Hockcliffe.

Grabbing her cloak and gloves, Brigham departed the cottage, slamming the door behind him but not bothering to replace the ledger in its place on the shelf.

He cared not a whit about the bloody accounts.

The only thing holding his attention and worthy of his time was Melloria.

Brigham pulled his reins free from the post and swung up onto his horse, driving his heels deep into the beast's sides as he took off in the direction of the manor. She couldn't have journeyed far on foot; however, glancing up, the sun had progressed in the sky.

How long had he wallowed in his self-pity?

Thundering across the field, he kept his eyes on the landscape and any sign of Mellie. He rode unheeded through crops and barren meadows without regard for anything but finding his wife. All the while, his chest burned, ached with the need for her forgiveness. Her understanding, though he was unworthy of either.

Hockcliffe came into view on the horizon, but Mellie was nowhere to be seen.

Had she gone in another direction? Was she out in the elements, freezing and in danger because Brigham had rebuffed her offer—her generous and selfless proposal?

Leaning low over his horse's neck, he prodded the beast forward, much as he'd rode into Hockcliffe the previous day.

Yet, the day before, he'd been riding headlong to get away from something. Today, he rode *toward* someone.

He should have never ridden away from her to begin with.

Brigham had leapt from his horse before the animal even stopped and ran for the door. If she weren't within, he would return to search for her.

Danvers pulled the door wide before Brigham reached the top step. "My lord. Is something amiss?"

"Your mistress, Mellie," he shouted. "Is she within?"

"Why, yes, I believe I caught sight of her scurrying up the servants' stairs not five minutes ago, my lord."

Brigham pushed past the servant only pausing to discard her cloak and gloves, ignoring the man's confusion and offer of assistance as he took the stairs three at a time until he strode down the hall that housed his room.

Though he did not continue to the large double doors at the end of the corridor; instead, he stopped before the entrance to Mellie's private chamber. He reached for the latch, prepared to throw the door open and rush inside, but he stilled his hand and took a deep breath. She'd arrived home safely, and there was no need to barge into her private quarters like a brute devoid of all manners.

Quashing his aggression, Brigham lifted his clenched fist and knocked.

Footsteps sounded inside as someone moved swiftly to answer the door.

As the door swung open on well-oiled hinges, he realized he'd never taken a step into her chambers before, nor so much as even looked past the threshold.

This day would be no different as he stared into the widened eyes of Lilly, Mellie's lady's maid.

Brigham stood mute, listening for any sign that Mellie was within.

"Yes, my lord?" Lilly dipped into a curtsey. "How can I be of service?"

Everyone in his household was offering him assistance, but he feared the situation had progressed too far for anyone to be of any help to him in his plight to secure his wife's forgiveness.

"My lord?"

"Mellie—Lady Whitmore—is she within?" His voice was gravelly as if he'd been crying... and perhaps he had. His anguish paled in comparison to the heartbreak he'd noted on Mellie's face before she fled the cottage. "Is she here? Where is your mistress?"

The servant shrank back into the room.

"She—she—she left this morn in pursuit of you, my lord."

"Are you certain you have not seen her since?"

"No, Lord Whitmore," the maid squeaked, placing her hand to her throat. "Did she not find you at the steward's cottage?" Concern flooded the servant's face, furrowing her brow.

How was he to admit to the women who'd watched over his wife when he was too much of a scoundrel to care for her properly that *he'd* wounded Mellie and caused her to flee in desperation?

CHAPTER 9

MELLIE GRASPED THE groom's proffered hand and stepped down from the carriage with Lilly close behind her as Danvers and Peter rushed from the manor to collect the pies, cheese, and fresh bread that the villagers had sent for their lord on this Christmastide eve.

She glanced about, determined to enter the house as she had after fleeing the cottage... unnoticed. Though, the distance and time—and urgency of the morning—was gone. No longer did tears streak her face, no longer were her eyes swollen from the wind and her sobs escaping her without notice as she'd ran across the meadow separating the steward's office and the manor, and not even the heat of his kiss lingered at her lips.

Poised and composed, with her emotions firmly in hand, Mellie would enter Hockcliffe as the mistress of the manor did. No one would be the wiser to her anguish from the morning.

It had been rather simple to avoid the

house—and Brigham—for the entirety of the day. Now would be no different. There had been matters in the kitchen to attend to, gifts to deliver to the children in the village, and now, with the full moon high above in the clear night sky, Mellie was nervous of seeing Brigham within the house. Certainly, he paced the corridors.

She'd heard him in the study when she snuck from the house earlier. His heavy footfalls pausing every ten paces before starting anew. If she closed her eyes, she could visualize him stalking from his desk to the door and back again. Thankfully, Lilly had let slip her mistress would be in the village most of the day and Brigham hadn't pursued her when her carriage left the manor.

If something weighed on his shoulders, he hadn't trusted her enough to speak of it… which was his right as a lord. Though their moments together in the cottage spoke much of a deeper connection between them, even if he fought against it. Even if he kept something from her, perhaps news from town, they could converse on other topics—namely, the passion they'd both nearly fallen prey to.

Instead, Brigham had pushed her away.

"I laid your evening gown out before we departed for the village," Lilly said at her side. "Shall I help you change and retire for the eve?"

Mellie glanced up at the clear night sky, the sun having set several hours before and the moon casting an almost enchanting shimmer on the landscape surrounding Hockcliffe.

"Do seek your own respite now." Mellie quickly embraced her maid and slipped her hands into her muff for warmth. "I think I will stroll the gardens before I return for my meal."

"It is dreadfully cold, my lady."

No colder than it would be in Brigham's presence.

"I will only remain outside for a short time. My word," she said with a smile. "This night… it is too beautiful to not enjoy, and the temperature is not so cold. Last year, if you remember, we had several feet of snow by this late date in December, and we didn't journey to the village with gifts until after the new year."

"You are correct, my lady."

Mellie dipped her head, in no way happy about being correct.

"I will bid you good night and see you when Christmastide morn is upon us." Lilly nodded and followed Danvers inside as he carried a platter of cheese made by Mrs. Confee.

"Good night," Mellie called after her.

No, she did not relish being correct about anything because that meant her suspicions regarding Brigham were correct. He'd created a life for himself in London, one that did not include Mellie, and he would return to town shortly. When next Christmastide season arrived, he'd fulfill his yearly obligation and venture to Hockcliffe for a few days' time before departing once again.

Straightening her shoulders, Mellie started for her garden reprieve, confident she would survive the muddled mess she'd made of her life. However, if she could not give Brigham an heir, her only other option was to free him to wed and love another.

The images of him holding another woman close, that woman running her fingers through his soft, curly hair, their lips locked together as hers and Brigham's had been only that very morning… Her knees shook as she walked, and she fought to banish the despondency that was already settling upon her.

She would not be reduced to tears—not over something she'd had a hand in creating.

The wind was a welcome balm to her overly warm face and neck, and she sucked in the frigid air, relishing the burn it caused within.

This was what she deserved—both for accepting Brigham's offer of marriage and condemning him to a loveless marriage, and for her blatant attempt to fool him into caring for her when his heart obviously belonged elsewhere.

How she wished she could return to before she'd wantonly thrown herself at him, and he'd rejected her advances. She'd been utterly wrong to think that after all these years there was any affection remaining between them. Without a doubt, she loved him—had always loved him—but to delude herself into believing he felt the same was ridiculous and childish. Even if a spark had developed between them once again, it was not so easy to forget their past and fall into lustful abandon.

Mellie kept close to the house as she made her way down the unlit path, careful to watch her footing to avoid tripping on any rocks or holes. It would not be wise to lose focus and stumble, injuring her ankle. Most of the servants had been given a night's leave to spend time with their families. No one would hear her calls for help, and she would likely perish from her death of cold before morning came.

It was not the servants' fault they had homes and families to attend to during the holidays.

Once, not long ago, Mellie had her own family, but with her mother gone, she was utterly alone these last several months.

She removed her hand from her muff and

placed it against the stone wall of the manor as she stepped over a tree limb that lay across her path. The moon overhead did its very best to light her way as she rounded the back of the house and slowly descended the cobblestone steps into the garden.

In its frozen, winterized state, the landscape paralleled her life.

Gone were the spring and summer blossoms of hope, and no promise of leaves to unfurl when the summer warmth once again returned were present as yet. With the Christmastide moon cascading over the garden, Mellie had the sense it would always remain thus: devoid of birds in the trees, shrubs that appeared more like a bunch of bundled sticks than a living plant, and the flower beds, abundant in the warmer months, nothing but frozen dirt.

It was as her life had been these last five years: barren, forlorn, and unmoving.

How had she not noticed the change as it had crept upon every aspect of her existence?

Even now, it was difficult to remember a time when she wasn't burdened with familial responsibilities, a time when she'd been young, untroubled, and eager to see what her future held.

One was not always blessed with choosing their fate or path in life.

There was no sense in bemoaning her hardships or dwelling on what could have been or how she should have lived her wedded life with Brigham.

What if she'd accepted his offer to accompany him to London?

It was the thought she attempted to keep unexplored.

However, this night, it was only Mellie, the moon overhead, and her musings.

In that moment, standing as husband and wife in this very garden, Mellie could have said yes. Arrangements could have been made to secure her mother's safe passage to town, Mellie and Brigham would have had more time to grow as one instead of establishing separate lives. Certainly, Brigham did not reside at his London townhouse every night, as he'd spoken at great length in the past about his many trips to grand estates all over England to discuss his reform bills with any and every influential lord who would lend an ear and backing.

Perhaps her mother would have been well enough for Mellie to accompany Brigham about the English countryside instead of remaining secluded at Hockcliffe.

She shook her head. There was little to be gained from dwelling on that which could not be changed.

Focusing on the garden around her, Mellie was surprised to see her feet had taken her to the exact spot where she and Brigham had become husband and wife. Viscount and Viscountess Whitmore.

Most days, she was still the pauper daughter of a lowly baron.

She'd never set about truly being Viscountess Whitmore.

Had she suspected all along that their marriage would meet this fate?

A gust of wind pulled at her hair, whipping it about her face before settling once more. Mellie tilted her head back and stared up at the full moon. How she wished she'd embraced change, like the passing phases of the moon, and not remained in her own personal frozen wasteland.

Perhaps after Brigham departed, she would move back to Tapton House, her family home. It had been left abandoned since her cousin drained the earth on her family lands and fled back to whence he came—where that was, Mellie had never cared. She had little resources beyond the dowry her father had established before his death. Would Brigham give her the funds? They wouldn't last long, but it might be enough to make it through a few years.

…and then what?

She'd lived for so long not thinking about what was to come on the morrow that, as of late, she couldn't find the willpower to live in the present.

The hour grew late, and the night chill settled about her. She should return to the house, seek out her meal, and find her bed.

A full night's rest might be enough to dim the sting awaiting her when Brigham announced his impending departure from Hockcliffe once more.

The snap of a twig had Mellie pivoting around toward the terrace, but the darkened space made it impossible to see what had caused the noise. Glancing upward, she noted a dim glow coming from the third-floor servants' quarters, but none from any of the lower two floors.

Had Brigham sought his own bed?

There was a certain lack of Christmastide cheer at Hockcliffe.

"Melloria?" His voice came from the darkness as if she'd conjured what her heart longed for, but that which her mind knew was not destined to be.

She scanned the midnight-kissed darkness

for him, the light from the moon suddenly dimming as if it sought to play games with her.

Brigham.

He was there, stepping from the shadows with a tiny, red-wrapped box in his outstretched hands.

Mellie remained where she was, making him journey the several paces to stand before her. She would not embarrass herself further by making this any more than it was. Brigham presented her with a simple Christmastide gift each year.

This year was to be no different, though Mellie's stomach hardened at the thought that this might very well be her last gift from him. She needed to set him free, give him her blessing to find happiness—wherever that may lie.

Maybe, in turn, she would find her own peace.

Not happiness, never that, but perchance contentment?

"My lord." Her voice was barely loud enough to hear over the subtle evening breeze.

Before her, Brigham was the man she'd known all her life, the man she'd given herself to in marriage, and the man who'd cared for her when her cousin cast her out.

He was kind, compassionate, and possessed an abundance of understanding.

Gone was the lord who'd pulled away from her embrace in anger that morning.

Mellie could not bring herself to believe that man and the one in front of her were one and the same.

"I have been searching for you all day."

Mellie glanced at her feet and willed her stomach to stop fluttering. He could have been seeking her out only to speak of his intentions to depart. "I was in the village delivering

Christmastide gifts."

"I would have accompanied you," he mumbled.

She brought her stare back to his, searching his face for any sign that the meaning of his words was not the same as what she heard. "I did not wish to disturb you."

His hands fumbled with the wrapped box he held between them as hers remained safely in her muff. "You have never, nor will you ever be a disturbance."

How she longed to believe him.

"What did you wish to speak with me about?" They might as well discuss things here and now. It was best to dispel the negative and start anew.

Yet, he remained silent, his gaze traveling over the garden around them. Did he take in the differences from when they'd stood in this spot before? Surely, he recognized the effect the harsh winter cold had had on the area.

When he finally spoke, it was not to say what he'd sought her out to discuss, Mellie was certain of that.

"You were exquisite that day we both stood here. You, in your long gown with blue blossoms held tightly, and me, far too afraid to speak for fear you'd change your mind and call off our marriage." He paused, glancing up at the moon. "Mellie, I agonized all afternoon about how we found ourselves in this position; you seeking to give me an heir because it was something you owed me, and me, so occupied all these years with trivial matters I neglected the woman I should hold above all else. When in fact, I was hiding myself away from you for fear you'd see how deeply my love for you ran."

"Love for me?" she stuttered. "Why would you need to hide such a thing from your wife?"

His imploring, honey brown eyes stared intensely at her. "Because I knew I would perish if I discovered you did not return my love."

"I would not have wed you if I did not love you, Brigham," Mellie confessed, while again pleading with her heart to slow its erratic pace.

He shook his head from side to side. "No, no, you did not wed me of your own free will. You know as well as I that my offer of marriage came at a time when you had no other options. Your mother was ill, your cousin had cast you out of Tapton House, and I swooped in and turned your misfortune into my gain."

"That is not the way of it, at all." Mellie slid her hands from her muff, and it fell to the ground at her feet, unnoticed, as she reached for his fingers still wrapped around the box. "Yes, I was blessed and fortunate to have you offer for my hand, but our match was already destined to be. At least in my mind." She swallowed, determined not to sob at what needed to be said next. "However, I am... overtaken with much remorse... for allowing our love to wither and die. I should have—"

His brow furrowed, and the pain in his eyes made it impossible for her to go on.

Perhaps enough had been said. This might be the best things could get between them.

"Nothing within me has withered and died, Melloria," he uttered. "My love for you has only grown over the years. It is I who has failed you."

He thought he failed her? She would not blame him if he'd taken a lover, nor would she cast a stone at him for deciding to depart Hockcliffe for good.

"Do not disparage yourself." Mellie dropped

her hands from his, her gaze following them and focusing on the toe of his Hessians. "It shall not reflect negatively on you if your heart now belongs to another. For many years, I was uncertain whether I had anything left within me to give."

"My heart has never and will never belong to another." His hand moved to tilt her chin up, but she pulled away as tears welled.

"It is only right and fair that you took a mistress."

He released her chin and stepped away. Was he shocked that she did not blame him for finding comfort in the arms of another?

"I would never dishonor my commitment to you, Melloria, especially by taking a mistress." The fury his voice held earlier returned.

"If not that, then how have you failed me?" Mellie's own temper rose, a spark of anger coiling within her.

"How have I *not* failed you?" He rubbed at his face with his free hand, notching his glasses askew. "I abandoned you on our wedding day. I stayed away during your mother's illness. I was not strong enough to return when she perished. And I have neglected you for years. I am an unfit man, not worthy of being noted as a gentleman." He pivoted away from her as he stared at the tiny package he still held. "And I was foolish enough to think that returning now, with a simple gift and a promise never to leave you again, would fix the damage that's already been done. Bloody hell. I had truly deluded myself into thinking all could be righted. I think it best if I depart Hockcliffe at first light in the morning."

And there it was, exactly as Mellie had feared it would be.

But unlike her pain at his yearly departures, something was different this time.

His words shattered something within her, causing a fracture that would never mend even after a thousand years.

This was both all she'd hoped for and everything she feared.

He'd declared his love for her.

And now he would leave her once more, but she had no reason to deceive herself into holding out hope he'd ever return again.

CHAPTER 10

HER WORDS WERE enough to bring him to his knees. She *had* loved him once, but he'd been too overcome by his own emotions to see it.

And he'd deserted her.

In a way, this was far more painful than hearing she'd never had affection for him at all.

A love left fallow was a waste for all.

Brigham turned toward the manor—his home…Mellie's home—and wondered how long it had taken for her love to subside. Perhaps she would share her secret to suppressing her love for him, and how long it would be until it faded enough to bare returning to his family home and seeing her.

"You have a gift for me?" Her soft voice by his ear had him turning back toward her, seeing her with fresh eyes, through the unclouded stare of a man who'd lived his entire adult life holding on to a thread of hope. "I should like to see it before you depart…if you must leave, that is."

That she still wanted anything he had to give her startled him nearly as much as her breath at his neck and the weight of her hand as it settled on his arm to halt him from fleeing the garden.

Brigham glanced down at the tiny box nestled in his hands. He'd selected the box with precise care and consideration, for it housed the Christmastide present that was to change their entire relationship. It had been meant to make amends for the past, speak of a new commitment for their present, and give them hope for the future to come.

Instead, it would be a parting gift.

"I had this commissioned especially for you, Mellie." He held the box out to her, begging himself to have the strength to watch her open it.

She took the gift and smiled up at him, her eyes clouded with tears.

The bright moon overhead made them glisten as they threatened to fall.

But then she was focused solely on the box, and her fingers shook as she removed the top to bring the pendant into view.

It was a simple adornment, as Mellie had never been one for garish jewels or gems.

Yet, it was made of the purest silver with a heart-shaped outer shell with wild blossoms encapsulating it. The pendant spoke of Mellie in a way no other necklace could. Quickly, she found the tiny, hidden clasp and released it, opening it to see inside. Two tiny images, barely decipherable in the night were nestled inside.

As if knowing the moment was a great turning point, the moon's rays brightened, casting a light like that of a close candle over the pair and illuminating two hand-drawn portraits; one of Mellie's parents, Baron and Baroness

Montfort, and on the opposite side, Mellie and Brigham on their wedding day.

"Oh, I had no idea these portraits existed," she sighed, her finger tracing first the likeness of her parents and then the one of she and Brigham. "Where did you…how did you…"

"I have always kept a painting of us with me. For the one of your parents, I went to Tapton House during the last Christmastide season and retrieved it."

When he'd journeyed to the neighboring estate the year before, it had been to assess the damage and repairs needed, but he'd found the portrait hidden in a corner of a dusty, abandoned chamber and he'd known he needed to take it. For what purpose, he hadn't been sure at the time.

However, seeing the smile on her lips, the sparkle in her green eyes, and the blossom of her complexion now was enough for him to know his choice of gift was perfect.

Though it hardly changed anything.

"May I?" Brigham held out his hand for the necklace. When she set the gift in his palm, she immediately turned around and lifted her hair for him to clasp the chain about her neck.

"It is beautiful, Brigham," her breathed as the weight settled on her bosom. "I shall cherish it always."

Why did her words hold such a powerful sting?

Because that was all she'd have to cherish, for he would be gone.

Before Brigham knew what was transpiring, he leaned forward and kissed her neck, following the trail of the pendant's chain as it cascaded over her shoulder, down to her clavicle, and to her cleavage where the heart lay.

"You are cold." Her skin was icy against his lips. "Let us return inside."

She turned to face him with agonizing slowness as she began to unbutton her cloak.

"The night is harsh, and I should retrieve your muff." Brigham glanced about, spotting her hand warmer on the ground several feet away.

He hurried over to collect it, and when he returned, she'd laid her long, flowing cloak on the ground—in the exact spot they promised to love and cherish one another for all their days.

The morning sun did not burn brightly in praise for their joining this night.

No, it was the Christmastide moon...full and casting its luminous glow over Mellie as she lowered herself to the cloak, her hair free about her shoulders and the pendant hanging between her breasts.

Never had Mellie been more stunning. Captivating. Utterly enchanting as she arranged her skirts about her on the ground.

But then...then she did the one thing that brought Brigham to his knees.

Mellie held out her hand to him.

It was a proposition.

She wanted Brigham to join her.

Under the Christmastide moon.

"Come, my husband."

There was so much left unsaid, hundreds of words he longed to say, though he could not find his voice as he sank to the ground beside her.

His wife.

The woman he'd lived all these years without, even though his heart had remained with her at Hockcliffe.

His entire body pulsed with need as she brushed his cheek with her hand before leaning in to set her lips upon his. This kiss was far different than their previous one at the cottage. That had been driven by a fiery need that had lain dormant between them for years. This kiss, this joining, went far deeper than pure lust, want, and desire.

Something inside Brigham reached out and took hold of Mellie, and he sensed it would always be that way. Denying his ever-present love for her, begging it to subside and recede, was futile.

Brigham pulled back as her brow furrowed in confusion.

There was much he needed to say, and this moment, this very intimate space of time, demanded he speak his piece.

"Mellie." He would not allow the words to come in a rush of mumbling, unintelligible utterances. She was worth more than a hastily spoken vow. "You must know I loved you the day we wed, and I've loved you every day since. My commitment to you has never wavered, though I have not been the husband you needed or deserved." When she made to close the distance between them and bring their lips back together, Brigham halted her. "I would not blame you if your love for me has waned over the years, as it was my own neglect of you and our marriage that caused the distance between us. However, from this day forward, even if your love for me never returns, I will remain by your side. Here at Hockcliffe or in London or even the great Sahara Desert. Wherever your heart leads you, I and my heart will follow. Anything you demand is yours."

His heart hammered in his chest as he fell silent. The cool night air only served to make

Brigham aware of the burning within him.

Mellie drew in a ragged breath. Her narrowed stare traveled no higher than the lapel of his coat as if she debated something.

"Do say something, please," Brigham pleaded. He lifted her chin with his forefinger, returning her stare to his. "Do not leave my mind adrift too long."

Yet, what he saw there was not confusion, puzzlement, or some great internal debate.

"Anything I demand?" Her lip turned up at the corner, and her eyes twinkled in the evening glow. "You will deny me nothing?"

Brigham swallowed hard past the lump in his throat. A nod was all he could muster in response to her question. He would walk to the ends of the Earth if she so demanded. He would rage a brutal war against anyone she named as foe. And he would give her any gift she longed to possess. All she need do is speak her command.

"Make love to me, Brigham." Her chin lifted as if daring him to deny her. "Bed me properly under the Christmastide moon."

She needn't command aught else as he pulled her close and set his lips to hers.

With ungainly coordination, Brigham reached behind her and untied the sash about her waist and then began with the buttons down her back—the same buttons he'd expertly undone just that morning.

Why was the task immensely more difficult now?

Every inch of him knew why, and he pulled back, needing Mellie to speak of it.

"I love you," he mumbled against her lips as she attempted to follow him.

Mellie paused, sensing what he asked of her.

"I loved you yesterday, I love you today, and I will love you even more tomorrow."

Holding her gaze, Brigham had no doubt that everything she spoke was the truth and rooted deep within her heart.

Swiftly, he moved through the buttons down the back of her gown.

Their labored breaths joined in the mere inches separating them and escaped into the night.

Mellie shrugged from the bodice of her gown, allowing it to pool at her waist, her thin shift barely hiding her hardened nipples.

His hand shook with desire when his finger grazed the tight bud, and he pushed the shoulders of her chemise down to follow the same path her bodice had taken.

Breathing deeply, Mellie's breasts rose and fell, her perfect form exposed to his ravenous stare.

He wanted to touch her, taste her, claim her.

When his stare returned to hers, Brigham had no doubt that she sought to do the same with him.

MELLIE HAD WAITED years for this moment. No, she'd waited a *lifetime* for Brigham to look at her as he was now. She wanted it to last decades; however, she also wanted his hands upon her bared breasts, his lips on her neck, and his manhood at her core.

Her need was her undoing.

Even without Brigham's declarations of love, she would have given him the gift of her body, her soul, her heart. No matter the outcome,

Mellie wanted their bodies joined this night, and she would not wait another moment.

Her body vibrated with need as her back arched, presenting her full, tight breasts for his touch; the magnificent necklace nestled between her mounds.

She recognized the instant his hesitation fled, and a flutter moved from her stomach to her throat as he reached forward and laid her back on the cloak. There were no words left within her, no need to speak…only act. Satiate the lust coursing through her.

Yet, he did not follow her, nor did Brigham lay beside her. He pushed to his feet and stood, his eyes never leaving hers as he slowly removed his jacket, untied his cravat, and began undoing the buttons of his white linen shirt until he ended at the flap of his trousers.

Mellie was helpless to stop herself as she licked at her lips, causing a low growl to escape from Brigham.

He tossed his glasses on the growing pile of clothing close to his feet, his shirt quickly following.

His Hessians were next, and then…his trousers.

She sucked in a deep breath, but it caught in her throat when she realized Brigham wore nothing under his trousers. His erection jutted out thickly and pulsed in the moonlight from above, his desire for her evident.

He was breathtaking as he continued to stand over her, his stare finally traveling down her body—giving her ample time to do the same with his. The sight of him did not assuage the need within her, however; it only amplified her arousal. Her fingers clawed at the cloak to keep from reaching for him.

Certainly, she wanted him stretched out beside her, on top of her, his lips against hers. But she was hesitant to end this speck in time. She'd never seen him thusly and she wanted to look her fill. Wanted to imprint on her memory the way he looked in the moonlight, a look of unabashed desire and need evident on his face. And love. Yes, there was love.

This was the moment in their lives every one to follow would be based on.

The longing in his eyes, the set of his broad shoulders, the intense line of his jaw.

Never again would she need fear what course her life would take, for Brigham would be ever at her side.

No lingering distress at being alone in the world could bring her to panic.

Brigham's confession began to take root. He was not leaving Hockcliffe—not this night, not on the morrow, or any day that followed...unless Mellie was with him.

"My dearest Lady Whitmore, I do hope—" He paused, his eyes dipping to take in her bare breasts. Mellie parted her thighs, primed for all that would come next. Feeling beautiful under his stare. "—you are prepared to be bedded under the Christmastide moon."

"It is the gift I've longed for since our wedding day," she purred, holding her arms wide.

He came to her then, in all of his naked glory, his scorching lips leaving a trail of raw, heated desire in their wake as he pushed her gown down over her hips and followed the path with his lips. When he paused, his lips pursed, Mellie knew a brief second of panic.

But instead of moving away, he lifted her

hips slightly and reached beneath her to untie the holds for her underskirts, pushing them down her thighs with the rest of her underthings.

The frosty night breeze that swept over her should have chilled her to the bone and numbed her, yet the sensation of his eyes upon her thrilled her senses to a new heightened awareness and heat bloomed anew at her core. A shudder ran down her spine at the thought of his tongue following the same path that his hands currently took. As if Brigham read her mind, he applied his lips to her naval and placed delicate kisses there.

His strong hands caressed the tight muscles of her thighs as he leaned over her, and her body liquefied under his ministrations. One hand massaged the weighty globe of a breast, coaxing a sigh from her lips, as the other trailed feather-light touches over her mound. Mellie felt heat pool at her core as Brigham stroked and played, kissed and nipped until she wanted to beg.

Mellie was gloriously exposed. She should be embarrassed, panicked, have an intense desire to cover her flesh; instead, she delighted in the sensations coursing through her. When he latched on to the sensitive area below her breast, her hands released their hold on the cloak and ran through his hair, locking tightly in his short curls and pulling him back to her lips.

A brief second of weight and heat hit her as Brigham shifted to lay between her spread thighs, the tip of his manhood finding her entrance much like a ship instinctively finds its place in the harbor.

Brigham, the man, was her home.

He'd always been her refuge, and there was no doubt he'd serve as her haven for all her years.

His eyes locked on hers—deepening to a liquid cocoa color—and then he entered her.

Gently at first, pausing to allow her to adjust to his size... and bloody hell, isn't that what he'd always done for her?

Her body gave way to him, tightening about his length as he slowly slid in and out, their natural connection creating a wave of warmth that surrounded them both, casting out the harsh December cold, and banishing their past to usher in their future.

That was Mellie's final thought before the world exploded around them as if the Christmastide moon had fallen to the ground, bringing the entire night sky with it... stars and all.

It was hours later, weeks later, years later, curled tight to Brigham's side, his body heat protecting her from the steadily dropping temperatures, that he placed a kiss to her forehead. Mellie cooed with contentment as she snuggled ever closer to his heat.

"Let us go inside," Brigham whispered, brushing her hair from his cheek to place his lips at the tender spot below her ear. "We have much to speak of, and I do not wish my lady to fall ill before our Christmastide morn—or before I have properly laid her at our wedded bed."

Searing heat still coursed through Mellie, the night frost solidly held at bay as long as Brigham was near—however, the comfort of a warm room was difficult to deny.

"Brigham—" Mellie swallowed the sob that threatened to escape. "My love for you has never waned... not for a moment."

"And it was thoughts of you that kept me sane all these years," he confessed, adjusting his position until he leaned on his elbow and stared directly into her eyes. "It was for *you* I've worked tirelessly to accomplish so much."

And accomplish much, they had, Mellie realized.

Brigham pushed to his feet, leaning down to lift her as he brought her cloak about her shoulder. With swift movements under the pale glow of the moon, he redressed and gathered her garments never removing his gaze from her. His intense stare kept her warm as if his hands were still on her body, caressing her hips, her thighs, her breasts.

Did he fear she would flee? Disappear? Make haste to the manor without him?

No, Mellie would not be going anywhere without Brigham.

Not today, tomorrow, or ever.

They'd been parted for far too long, however, after this night, Mellie vowed never a moment should pass with her dearest husband removed from her.

Whether it be under the Christmastide moon with the stars shining bright, only her cloak to protect them or beneath the canopy of their marriage bed, wrapped in blankets of the softest velveteen, Brigham would be at her side.

AUTHOR'S NOTES

Thank you for reading *Bedded by the Christmastide Moon!* If you enjoyed this book, be sure to write a brief review at any retailer.

I'd love to hear from you!
You can contact me at:
Christina@christinamcknight.com
Or write me at:
P.O. Box 1017
Patterson, CA 95363

www.ChristinaMcKnight.com
Check out my website for giveaways, book reviews, and information on my upcoming projects,
or connect with me through social media at:
Twitter: @CMcKnightWriter
Facebook:
www.facebook.com/christinamcknightwriter
Goodreads:
www.goodreads.com/ChristinaMcKnight

Sign up for my newsletter here:
http://eepurl.com/VP1rP

Turn the page for an excerpt from
Bound by the Christmastide Moon,
where two strangers find love under the glowing moon of the Cornwall shore!

Ditchley Hall, Southampton, England
June 1811

SILAS ANSON, THE eighth Earl of Lichfield, glared across the vast, disorderly expanse of what he'd recently come to view as *his* desk, not the unfamiliar, cluttered stretch of flat surface that had once belonged to his father.

A man he barely remembered and could not conjure in his mind.

On the receiving end of Silas's scowl was none other than Mr. Horace Peabody, Esquire.

The solicitor had also come with the Lichfield title and estate.

Though Silas silently debated which was of lesser value to him: his non-existent heritage or his father's trusted advisor.

"You are telling me—" Silas clamped his mouth shut, pondering and discarding his next statement as overly crass and unwarranted, no matter the validity of it. "You are telling me I was summoned back to England, ripped from my home in France, to inherit a title and estate so entrenched in debt that ruination can only be staved off for a month's time?"

Mr. Peabody, who surprisingly in no way resembled a pea of any sort, stared mutely at Silas from behind his rounded spectacles, his hands clenched on the stack of folders in his lap. Did the man realize how cliché he appeared? Glasses, ink-stained fingers, nerves so frazzled he shook, and the piles of paperwork. Lord above, the man had arrived with an entire forest's worth of the stuff. One could only imagine the mines exploited to collect the graphite needed to scribble all the nonsense that'd been presented to Silas.

And the solicitor had appeared anxious since his arrival.

"This plan you've so graciously detailed for me is the only viable option you have been able to ascertain for rescuing the Lichfield name?" Silas needed to hear Peabody verbalize his recommended course one last time; but the solicitor only nodded, his glasses slipping down the bridge of his nose. Silas wondered if he shouldn't seek other counsel in this matter—and every matter to come. "My estate is bankrupt, the title worthless, and my only recourse—if I refuse to throw myself at the mercy of my mother's family—is as outlined on this single sheet of paper?"

To further punctuate the absurdity of the situation, Silas retrieved the aforementioned document with its hastily written paragraph and held it high for Peabody to inspect.

"That is, indeed, my recommendation, my lord," Peabody croaked, bowing his head.

If his father were not solidly in his grave, Silas would do away with the previous earl himself.

Bloody damnation, but Silas—along with his mother and siblings—had been content and otherwise entertained in Paris all these years. That was before he'd been unceremoniously summoned back to his father's homeland to usurp a title he'd never thought to possess.

Silas slumped in his seat and scrubbed his face, attempting to gain some clarity on the situation—yet, it eluded him still.

His mother, Mary Louisa Anson, Lady Lichfield, had absconded from England over fifteen years prior, her three young children in tow, never to see her husband again. Edmond Anson hadn't come looking for his family, hadn't sent so much as a messenger to check on their whereabouts or safety, nor the authorities to return his offspring to their rightful place in England.

As the years passed and no one came for them, Silas and his siblings adjusted to life in France as their mother pursued her passion for art. He'd assumed his father had forged a new life and continued as if his twin sons and young daughter had never existed.

The solicitor perked up, a new spark of hope

lighting his otherwise lackluster stare. "You can always reach out to Mrs. Hambly. I have heard she is a fair woman who loves her relations. Do not so readily cast her—and your other aunts—aside. Perhaps the Countess of Somerton will be willing to step in and assist—"

Silas snorted. Yes, he'd been regaled with tales of the formidable Regina, his mother's sister, for years, and none of them spoke to her fair nature or love for her family, but rather to her need to be in control. "If my aunt cared a whit for her *relations*, she would have pursued my mother and offered assistance. Yet, my siblings and I lived on little more but stale bread and broth for years, residing above a butcher's shop in an unsavory part of Paris." Silas would not go into detail about the horrid conditions of his childhood—not with this man, at least. "No, that is not an option, at least not at this juncture."

"My plan will only solve a fraction of your problems, my lord." Peabody sighed, glancing toward the closed door of the study, his wide stare begging for any interruption as a means for escape. "And the solution itself is only temporary, at best."

"How could my father allow his estate to fall into such shambles?" Silas mused, expecting no answer, for any retort would not satisfy him.

"Because he was heartbro—" The solicitor's words cut short, and he swallowed. The tall clock chimed four times, echoing through the cavernous corridors of Ditchley Hall. "If there is nothing else you require, I will see myself out and prepare to depart for London."

Peabody stood, his lean, lanky body spoke of a man trapped behind a desk in a moldy room for over half his day, his pale skin in desperate need of sunlight.

Silas wanted the man gone, out of his office and away from Ditchley altogether. Away before word traveled to his siblings about the dire state of their affairs. Yet, that would not improve his family's situation nor hold the creditors at bay for long.

"Sit." His command reverberated off the walls and shook the windowpanes, sending a shiver down his spine. That was one positive of Ditchley Hall: his voice was a fearsome sound in every room. "I wish to speak further about my course for the next several months if I entertain your plan."

Regaining his seat, the solicitor shuffled through his folders in search of something, likely the means to keep Silas's wrath at bay a bit longer.

"An arranged marriage…"

"Yes, Lord Lichfield," Peabody nodded. "My notion to rescue the estate—at least for the time being—and keep your name and that of your siblings from the gossip mills, is to secure a mutually beneficial match."

"Mutually beneficial?" Silas had never envisioned himself wedded, especially after his parents' disastrous match. The only ones to suffer were the children of Edmond and Mary Louisa Anson. "What have I to offer a woman with a healthy enough dowry to sustain Ditchley Hall and provide for my siblings' immediate futures?"

Silas was speaking in questions once again, yet, when a man had no answers of consequence, all that was left was questions.

His entire life since fleeing England had been about finding answers…solutions to the many looming problems that plagued his family. When his mother had embraced her creative ways once across the Channel and neglected her children's upbringing, it had been up to Silas to find the means to educate his siblings, Slade and Sybil. He'd spent countless hours at the *Bibliothèque nationale de France*, first teaching himself to read, and then returning to their meager flat with the tomes necessary to instruct his brother and sister.

"You have a generations-old—and might I add, respected—title with connections to far more powerful members of society." Peabody recited the line as if he'd practiced it the entire journey from London. "That being said, I do not think it wise, or advantageous in your precarious position, to speak of the strained ties between you and your most notable relations."

Silas fairly growled. "Do you think me foolish enough to begin every conversation with the scandalous details of my mother's banishment?"

The solicitor's gaze swung back to Silas, his brow furrowed. "Your mother—errr, Lady Lichfield—was not banished. Has never been spoken of in anything but the highest regard by my employer, I mean to say, the previous Lord Lichfield...your father." Peabody held up a single finger as he riffled through his papers once more. "Ah, yes, here it is. Your father commissioned this letter in the event that your mother returned to England after his death. It states that in accordance with British law, she is, always has been, and will remain, Lady Lichfield. While you are the Lichfield heir, your mother is entitled to a hefty allowance and an estate, if she so chooses to accept it."

Chooses to accept it.

Most peculiar phrasing, indeed.

"I'm assuming this has the stipulation that it is only enforceable after my father's death." The statement drew another uneasy glance from the solicitor, and bloody hell if Silas wasn't remorseful over his lack of enthusiasm to review the piles of paperwork littering his desk. "Because there is no other reason *my father* would have allowed his *family* to live in squalor in Paris if there were funds and property set aside for my mother."

The solicitor once again focused on the folder before him, flipping pages until he found what he searched for. He lowered his head further, his lips moving as he read. "There is no such clause, my lord."

"Then why—" Silas stopped himself once more, knowing his fury would find no peace by harming the messenger. There was little use demanding to understand the inner workings of his late father. "Let us return to your original plan."

"Very good, my lord." The man's head bobbed up and down, obviously aware he'd avoided Silas's displeasure for the time being. "I have it all written down before you."

"Yes, however, there seems to be one crucial flaw."

"Oh?" the solicitor asked, leaning forward over his stack of papers to see the page on Silas's desk. "What would that be?"

Silas snatched the document and held it before him. "It details my need to wed—and marry for a healthy dowry—however, it does not purport *whom*, precisely, I should espouse." When the solicitor remained silent, he continued. "Being new to society, you should be well *aware* I am blissfully *unaware* of whom, exactly, has a sizeable dowry—and who will only bring increased hardship to the Lichfield name."

"I would never seek to command you in

whom to wed, my lord."

Odd, as the man had sent numerous correspondences about what was needed to keep the earldom afloat for another quarter.

Silas massaged his temples as he eyed the solicitor.

Would anyone truly miss the incompetent man if he were not to make it back to London?

Yet, he must needs remember he was in England once more, not the uncivilized country of France—as most Englishmen were fond to classify those who chose to live across the Channel.

"By chance have you any *suggestions* for proper, financially well-endowed ladies I should seek to court?"

Peabody broke into a broad smile as if Silas had finally asked the exact question he'd been waiting to hear. "I happen to have a client who…"

"How very fortunate…"

"Yes, well, he is not actively seeking a marriage for his daughter but has sought my advice on several occasions in regards to finding a match for her."

"Her worth?"

"Pardon?" Peabody said with a gulp.

"What is her worth? If I am to sell myself to the highest bidder, I would know the reward is sufficient to see me through for several years." Silas would never entertain a union unless he reaped adequate benefits: funds enough to see his siblings accepted into society, and prestige to overshadow his mother's estranged family. "Also, I suppose I should hear what you know of the girl."

"Her dowry is sufficient if you adhere to my other advice on managing your estate and investing in appropriately modest ventures. The woman in question is the only daughter of a marquess—a wealthy and connected marquess. If you have aspirations for the House of Lords, he will be an admirable advocate."

"I have never seen myself as a political man."

"Then, perhaps, you will be more in line with her brother. He is an earl and quite the man about town. A confirmed rakehell with an untouchable reputation in business, and a propensity for the gaming tables."

This earl seemed more suited as a friend for Slade, as opposed to an ally for Silas. "I would have the family name."

"The Marquess and Marchioness of Blandford." The solicitor again searched his paper, his finger running down the page until he found what he sought. "Their daughter, aged eighteen summers, is Lady Mallory Hughes."

Silas only hoped the woman did not have a third eye—or worse, the facial hair of a man. Silas supposed the son of a flighty countess could not expect much on his return to England, and the advantages of the match certainly outweighed the negatives. He needed money and means to see him and his siblings settled among the *ton*. Things that his father hadn't seen fit to provide.

"You will handle the paperwork?" Silas inquired, his brow rising in challenge.

"Without a doubt, my lord." Peabody pushed to his feet again, clutching his folders to his narrow chest as the stack threatened to escape and cascade to the floor. "I will write him at once upon my return to London. I am certain he will entertain the match."

Silas remained seated as Peabody scurried

from the room. Odd a man of such height and thin frame could scurry, but that he did. With any luck, the solicitor would arrive in London and secure the proper paperwork within a fortnight.

The grandfather clock chimed once more — five loud gongs, echoing through the house, reminding Silas he was to meet his siblings in the grand hall for supper.

ABOUT THE AUTHOR

USA TODAY Bestselling Author Christina McKnight writes emotional and intricate Regency Romance with strong women and maverick heroes.

Her books combine romance and mystery, exploring themes of redemption and forgiveness. When she's not writing, Christina enjoys trying new coffeehouses, visiting wine bars, traveling the world, and watching television.

Email: Christina@ChristinaMcKnight.com
Follow her on Twitter: @CMcKnightWriter
Keep up to date on her releases:
www.christinamcknight.com
Like Christina's FB Author page:
ChristinaMcKnightWriter

www.ingramcontent.com/pod-product-compliance
Lightning Source LLC
Chambersburg PA
CBHW030558130626
46552CB00006B/2596